A
is for
Alien

A
is for
Alien

CAITLÍN R. KIERNAN

Subterranean Press • 2009

Publication History

"Riding the White Bull" Copyright © 2004. First published in *Argosy
Magazine* #1, January/February 2004, edited by Lou Anders, Coppervale
International.

"Zero Summer" Copyright © 2007. First published in *Subterranean
Magazine* #6, edited by William K. Schafer, Subterranean Press.

"Faces in Revolving Souls" Copyright © 2005. First published in *Outsiders*,
edited by Nancy Holder and Nancy Kilpatrick, New American Library.

"In View of Nothing," Copyright © 2007. First print publication.

"The Pearl Diver" Copyright © 2006. First published in *Futureshocks*,
edited by Lou Anders, New American Library.

"A Season of Broken Dolls" Copyright © 2007. First print publication

"Ode to Katan Amano" Copyright © 2005. First published in *Frog Toes and
Tentacles*, Subterranean Press.

"Bradbury Weather" Copyright © 2005. First Published in *Subterranean
Magazine* #2, edited by William K. Schafer, Subterranean Press.

First Edition

ISBN
978-1-59606-209-2

Subterranean Press
PO Box 190106
Burton, MI 48519

www.subterraneanpress.com

Author's websites:
caitlinrkiernan.com
greygirlbeast.livejournal.com
myspace.com/greygirlbeast

Table of Contents

For my mother, Susan Ramey Cleveland (née, Susan Elaine Ramey), who introduced me to the work of Ray Bradbury, Harlan Ellison, Theodore Sturgeon, Kurt Vonnegut, and so many others who have influenced my writing. She also took me to see Kubrick's *2001: A Space Odyssey* when I was five years old and could not yet possibly hope to understand it.

It left a rather nice scar, regardless.

We live on a placid island of ignorance in the midst of the black seas of infinity, and it is not meant that we should voyage far.

—H. P. Lovecraft

Shame on us, doomed from the start.
May God have mercy on our dirty little hearts.
Shame on us for all we have done.
And all we are worth is just zeroes and ones.

—NIN

Riding the White Bull

Y ou've been drinking again, Mr. Paine," Sarah said, and I suppose I must have stopped whatever it was I was doing, probably staring at those damned pics again, the ones of the mess the cops had turned up that morning in a nasty little dump on Columbus—or maybe chewing at my fingernails, or thinking about sex. Whatever. Something or another that suddenly didn't matter anymore because she wasn't asking me a question. Sarah rarely had time for questions. She just wasn't that sort of a girl anymore. She spoke with a directness and authority that would never match her pretty artificial face, and that dissonance, that absolute betrayal of expectation, always made people sit up and listen. If I'd been looking at the photos—I honestly can't remember—I probably laid them down again and looked at her, instead.

"There are worse things," I replied, which I suppose I thought was some sort of excuse or defense or something, but she only scowled at me and shook her head.

"Not for you there aren't," she whispered, speaking so low that I almost couldn't make out the words over the faint hum of her metabolic servos and the rumble of traffic down on the street. She blinked and turned away, staring out my hotel window at the dark gray sky hanging low above the Hudson. The snow had finally stopped falling and the clouds had an angry, interrupted intensity to them. Jesus. I can remember the fucking clouds, can even assign them human emotions, but I can't remember what I was doing when Sarah told me I was drinking again. The bits we save, the bits we throw away. Go figure.

"The Agency doesn't need drunks on its payroll, Mr. Paine. The streets of New York are full of drunks and junkies. They're cheaper than rat shit. The Agency needs men with clear minds."

Sarah had a way of enunciating words so that I knew they were capitalized. And she always capitalized Agency. Always. Maybe it was a glitch in one of her language programs, or, then again, maybe she just made me paranoid. Sarah and the booze and the fucking Agency and, while I'm on the subject, February in Manhattan. By that point, I think I'd have given up a couple of fingers and a toe to be on the next flight back to LA.

"We hired you because Fennimore said you were sober. We checked your records with the Department of-"

"Why are you *here*, Sarah? What do you want? I have work to do," and I jabbed a thumb at the cluttered desk on the other side of my unmade bed. "Work for you and the Agency."

"Work you can't do drunk."

"Yeah, so why don't you fire my worthless, intoxicated ass and put me on the next jump back to Los Angeles? After this morning, I honestly couldn't give a shit."

"You understood, when you took this job, Mr. Paine, that there might be exceptional circumstances."

She was still staring out the window towards the sludgy, ice-jammed river and Jersey, an almost expectant expression on her face, the sullen winter light reflecting dull and iridescent off her unaging dermafab skin.

"We were quite explicit on that point."

"Of course you were," I mumbled, half to myself, even less than half to the cyborg who still bothered to call herself Sarah, and then I stepped around the foot of the bed and sat down on a swivel-topped aluminum stool in front of the desk. I made a show of shuffling papers about, hoping that she'd take the hint and leave. I needed a drink and time alone, time to think about what the hell I was going to do next. After the things I'd seen and heard, the things in the photographs I'd taken, the things they wouldn't *let* me photograph, I was beginning to understand why the Agency had decided not to call an alert on this one, why they were keeping the CDC and BioCon and the WHO in the dark. Why they'd called in a scrubber, instead.

"It'll snow again before morning," Sarah said, not turning away from the window.

"If you can call that crap out there snow," I replied, impatiently. "It's not even white. It smells like...fuck, I don't know what it smells like, but it doesn't smell like snow."

"You have to learn to let go of the past, Mr. Paine. It's no good to you here. No good at all."

"Is that Agency policy?" I asked, and Sarah frowned.

"No, that's not what I meant. That's not what I meant at all." She sighed then, and I wondered if it was just habit or if she still needed to breathe, still needed oxygen to drive the patchwork alchemy of her biomechs. I also wondered if she still had sex and, if so, with what. Sarah and I had gone a few rounds, way back in the day, back when she was still one-hundred percent flesh and blood, water and bone and cartilage. Back when she was still scrubbing freelance, before the Agency gave her a contract and shipped her off to the great frozen dung heap of Manhattan. Back then, if anyone had asked, I'd have said it was her life, her decisions to make, and a girl like Sarah sure as fuck didn't need someone like me getting in her way.

"I was trying to say—here, now—we have to live in the present. That's all we have."

"Forget it," I told her, glancing up too quickly from the bloody, garish images flickering across the screen of my old Sony-Akamatsu laptop. "Thanks for the ride, though."

"No problem," Sarah whispered. "It's what I do," and she finally turned away from the window, the frost on the Plexiglas, the wide interrupted sky.

"If I need anything, I'll give you or Templeton a ring," I said and Sarah pretended to smile, nodded her head and walked across the tiny room to the door. She opened it, but paused there, one foot across the threshold, neither in nor out, the heavy, cold air and flat fluorescent lighting from the hallway leaking in around her, swaddling her like a second-rate halo.

"Try to stay sober," she said. "Please. Mr. Paine. This one… it's going to be a squeeze." And her green-brown eyes shimmered faintly, those amazing eight-mill-a-pair spheres of fiber-optic filament and scratch-resistant acrylic, tinted mercury suspension-platinum lenses and the very best circuitry German optimetrics had figured out how to cram into a 6.5 cc socket. I imagined, then or only later on—that's something else I can't remember— that the shimmer stood for something Sarah was too afraid to say aloud, or something the Agency's behavioral inhibitors wouldn't allow her to say, something in her psyche that had been stamped Code Black, Restricted Access.

"Please," she said again.

"Sure. For old time's sake," I replied.

"Whatever it takes, Mr. Paine," and she left, pulling the door softly closed behind her, abandoning me to my dingy room and the dingier afternoon light leaking in through the single soot-streaked window. I listened to her footsteps on the tile, growing fainter as she approached the elevator at the other end of the hall, and when I was sure she wasn't coming back, I reached for the half-empty bottle of scotch tucked into the shadows beneath the edge of the bed.

Back then, I still dreamed about Europa every fucking night. Years later, after I'd finally been retired by the Agency and was only Dietrich Paine again, pensioned civilian has-been rotting away day by day by day in East LA or NoHo or San Diego—I moved around a lot for a drunk—a friend of a friend's croaker hooked me up with some black-market head tweaker. And he slipped a tiny silver chip into the base of my skull, right next to my metencephalon, and the bad dreams stopped, just like that. No more night flights, no more cold sweats, no more screaming until the neighbors called the cops.

But that winter in Manhattan, I was still a long, long decade away from the tweaker and his magic silver chip, and whenever the insomnia failed me and I dozed off for ten or fifteen or twenty minutes, I was falling again, tumbling silently through the darkness out beyond Ganymede, falling towards that Great Red Spot, that eternal crimson hurricane, my perfect, vortical Hell of phosphorus-stained clouds. Always praying to whatever dark Jovian gods might be watching my descent that *this* time I'd sail clear of the moons and the anti-cyclone's eye would swallow me at last, dragging me down, burning me, crushing me in that vast abyss of gas and lightning and infinite pressure. But I never made it. Not one single goddamn time.

"Do you believe in sin?" Sarah would ask me, when she was still just Sarah, before the implants and augmentations, and I would lie there in her arms, thinking that I was content, and stare up at the ceiling of our apartment and laugh at her.

"I'm serious, Deet."

"You're always serious. You've got serious down to an exact science."

"I think you're trying to avoid the question."

"Yeah, well, it's a pretty silly fucking question."

"Answer it anyway. Do you believe in sin?"

There's no way to know how fast I'm moving as I plummet towards the hungry, welcoming storm, and then Europa snags me. *Maybe next time*, I think. *Maybe next time.*

"It's only a question," Sarah would say. "Stop trying to make it anything more than that."

"Most of us get what's coming to us, sooner or later."

"That's not the same thing. That's not what I asked you."

And the phone would ring, or I'd slip my hand between her unshaven legs, or one of our beepers would go off, and the moment would melt away, releasing me from her scrutiny.

It never happened exactly that way, of course, but who's keeping score?

In my dreams, Europa grows larger and larger, sprouting from the darkness exactly like it did in the fucking orientation vids every scrubber had to sit through in those days if he or she wanted a license. Snippets of video from this or that probe borrowed for my own memories. Endless fractured sheets of ice the color of rust and sandstone, rising up so fast, so fast, and I'm only a very small speck of meat and white EMU suit streaking north and east across the ebony skies above Mael Dúin, the Echion Linea, Cilix, the southeastern terminus of the Rhadamanthys Linea. I'm only a shooting star hurtling along above that terrible varicose landscape, and I can't remember how to close my eyes.

"Man, I was right fucking there when they opened the thing," Ronnie says again and takes another drag off her cigarette. Her hand trembles and ash falls to the Formica tabletop. "I'd asked to go to Turkey, right, to cover the goddamn war, but I pulled the IcePIC assignment instead. I was waiting in the pressroom with everyone else, watching the feed from the quarantine unit when the sirens started."

"The Agency denies you were present," I reply as calmly as I can, and she smiles that nervous, brittle smile she always had, laughs one of her dry, humorless laughs, and gray smoke leaks from her nostrils.

"Hell, I know that, Deet. The fuckers keep rewriting history so it always comes out the way they want it to, but I was there, man. I *saw* it, before they shut down the cameras. I saw all that shit that 'never happened'," and she draws quotation marks in the air with her index fingers.

That was the last time I talked to Ronnie, the last time I visited her out at La Casa Psychiatric, two or three weeks before she hung herself with an electrical cord. I went to the funeral, of course. The Agency sent a couple of black-suited spooks with carefully-worded condolences for her family, and I ducked out before the eulogy was finished.

And here, a few kilometers past the intersection of Tectamus Linea and Harmonia Linea, I see the familiar scatter of black dots laid out helter-skelter on the crosscut plains. "Ice-water volcanism," Sarah whispers inside my helmet; I know damn well she isn't there, hasn't been anywhere near me for years and years, and I'm alone and only dreaming her voice to break the deafening weight of silence. I count the convection cells like rosary beads, like I was ever Catholic, like someone who might have once believed in sin. I'm still too far up to see any evidence of the lander, so I don't know which hole is The Hole, Insertion Point 2071A, the open sore that Emmanuel Weatherby-Jones alternately referred to as "the plague gate" and "the mouth of Sakpata" in his book on the Houston incident and its implications for theoretical and applied astrobiology. I had to look that up, because he never explained who or what Sakpata was. I found it in an old book on voodoo and Afro-Caribbean religions. Sakpata is a god of disease.

I'm too far up to guess which hole is Sakpata's mouth and I don't try.

I don't want to know.

A different sort of god is patiently waiting for me on the horizon.

"They started screaming," Ronnie says. "Man, I'll never forget that sound, no matter how many pills these assholes feed me. We all sat there, too fucking stunned to move, and this skinny little guy from CNN—"

"Last time he was from *Newsweek*," I say, interrupting her, and she shakes her head and takes another drag, coughs and rubs at her bloodshot eyes.

"You think it makes any goddamned difference?"

"No," I reply dishonestly, and she stares at me for a while without saying anything else.

"When's the last time you got a decent night's sleep?" she asks me, finally, and I might laugh, or I might shrug, and "Yeah," she says. "That's what I thought."

She starts rattling on about the hydrobot, then, the towering black smokers, thermal vents, chemosynthesis, those first grainy snatches of video, but I'm not listening. I'm too busy zipping helplessly along above buckled Europan plains and vast stretches of blocky, shattered chaos material; a frozen world caught in the shadow of Big Daddy Jupiter, frozen for ages beyond counting, but a long fucking way from dead, and I would wake up screaming or crying or, if I was lucky, too scared to make any sound at all.

"They're ready for you now, Mr. Paine," the cop said, plain old NYPD street blue, and I wondered what the fuck he was doing here, why the Agency was taking chances like that. Probably the same poor bastard who'd found the spooch, I figured. Templeton had told me that someone in the building had complained about the smell and, so, the super buzzed the cops, so this was most likely the guy who answered the call. He might have a partner around somewhere. I nodded at him, and he glanced nervously back over his shoulder at the open door to the apartment, the translucent polyurethane iso-seal curtain with its vertical black zipper running right down the middle, all the air hoses snaking in and out of the place, keeping the pressure inside lower than the pressure outside. I doubted he would still be breathing when the sweeper crews were finished with the scene.

"You see this sort of shit very often?" he asked, and it didn't take a particularly sensitive son of a bitch to hear the fear in his voice, the fear and confusion and whatever comes after panic. I didn't respond. I was busy checking the batteries in one of my cameras and, besides, I had the usual orders from Templeton to keep my mouth shut around civvies. And knowing the guy was probably already good as dead, that he'd signed his death warrant just by showing up for work that morning, didn't make me particularly eager to chat.

"Well, I don't mind telling you, I've never seen shit like that thing in there," he said and coughed. "I mean, you see some absolutely fucked-up shit in this city, and I even did my four years in the army—hell, I was in fucking Damascus after the bomb, but holy Christ Almighty."

"You were in Damascus?" I asked, but didn't look up from my equipment, too busy double-checking the settings on the portable genetigraph clipped to my belt to make eye contact.

"Oh yeah, I was there. I got to help clean up the mess when the fires burned out."

"Then that's something we have in common," I told him and flipped my vidcam's ON switch and the gray LED screen showed me five zeros. I was patched into the portable lab down on the street, a black Chevy van with Maryland plates and a yellow ping-pong ball stuck on the antenna. I knew Sarah would be in the van, waiting for my feed, jacked in, riding the amps, hearing everything I heard, seeing everything I saw through her perfectly calibrated eyes.

"You were in Syria?" the cop asked me, glad to have something to talk about besides what he'd seen in the apartment.

"No, I clean up other people's messes."

"Oh," he said, sounding disappointed. "I see."

"Had a good friend in the war, though. But he was stationed in Cyprus, and then the Taurus Mountains."

"You ever talk with him? You know, about the war?"

"Nope. He didn't make it back," I said, finally looking up, and I winked at the cop and stepped quickly past him to the tech waiting for me at the door. I could see she was sweating inside her hazmat hood, even though it was freezing in the hallway. Scrubbers don't get hazmat suits. It interferes with the contact, so we settle for a couple of hours in decon afterwards, antibiotics, antitox, purgatives, and hope we don't come up red somewhere down the line.

"This is bad, ain't it?" the cop asked. "I mean, this is something *real* bad," and I didn't turn around, just shrugged my shoulders as the tech unzipped the plastic curtain for me.

"Is that how it looked to you?" I replied. I could feel the gentle rush of air into the apartment as the slit opened in front of me.

"Jesus, man, all I want's a straight fucking answer," he said. "I think I deserve that much. Don't you?" and since I honestly couldn't say one way or the other, since I didn't even care, I ignored him and stepped through the curtain into this latest excuse for Hell.

There's still an exhibit at the American Museum of Natural History, on the fourth floor with the old Hall of Vertebrate Origins and all the dinosaur bones. The Agency didn't shut it down after the first outbreaks, the glory spooches that took out a whole block in Philadelphia and a trailer park somewhere in West Virginia, but it's not as popular as you might think. A dark, dusty alcove crowded with scale models and dioramas, videos monitors running clips from the IcePIC's hydrobot, endless black and white loops of gray seafloors more than half a billion kilometers from earth. When the exhibit first opened, there were a few specimens on loan from NASA, but those were all removed a long time ago. I never saw them for myself, but an acquaintance on staff at the museum, a geologist, assures me they were there. A blue-black bit of volcanic rock sealed artfully in a Lucite pyramid, and two formalin-filled specimen canisters, one containing a pink worm-like organism no more than a few centimeters in length, the other preserving one of the ugly little slugs that the mission scientists dubbed "star minnows."

"Star leeches" would have been more accurate.

On Tuesday afternoon, the day after I'd worked the scene on Columbus, hung over and hoping to avoid another visit from Sarah, I took the B-Line from my hotel to the museum and spent a couple of hours sitting on a bench in that neglected alcove, watching the video clips play over and over again for no one but me.

Three monitors running simultaneously—a NASA documentary on the exploration of Europa, beginning with Pioneer 10 in 1973, a flyover of the moon's northern hemisphere recorded shortly before the IcePIC orbiter deployed its probes, and a snippet of film shot beneath the ice. That's the one I'd come to see. I chewed aspirin and watched as the hydrobot's unblinking eyes peered through veils of silt and megaplankton, into the interminable darkness of an alien ocean, the determined glare of the bot's lights never seeming to reach more than a few feet into the gloom. Near the end of the loop, you get to see one of the thermal vents, fringed with towering sulfide chimneys spewing superheated, methane- and hydrogen-rich water into the frigid Europan ocean. In places, the sides of the chimneys were completely obscured by a writhing, swaying carpet of creatures. Something like an eel slipped unexpectedly past the camera lens. A few seconds later, the seafloor was replaced by a brief stream of credits and then the NASA logo before the clip started itself over again.

I tried hard to imagine how amazing these six minutes of video must have seemed, once upon a time, how people must have stood in lines just to see it, back before the shit hit the fan and everyone everywhere stopped wanting to talk about IcePIC and its fucking star minnows. Before the government axed most of NASA's exobiology program, scrapped all future missions Europa, and cancelled plans to explore Titan. Back before ET became a four-letter word. But no matter how hard I tried, all I could think about was that thing on the bed, the crap growing from the walls of the apartment and dripping from the goddamn ceiling.

In the museum, above the monitor, there was a long quote from H. G. Wells printed in red-brown ink on a clear Lexan plaque, and I read it several times, wishing that I had a cigarette—"We look back through countless millions of years and see the great will to live struggling out of the intertidal slime, struggling from shape to shape and from power to power, crawling and then walking confidently upon the land, struggling generation after generation to master the air, creeping down into the darkness of the deep; we see it turn upon itself in rage and hunger and reshape itself anew, we watch it draw nearer and more akin to us, expanding, elaborating itself, pursuing its relentless inconceivable purpose, until at last it reaches us and its being beats through our brains and arteries."

I've never cared very much for irony. It usually leaves a sick, empty feeling in my gut. I wondered why no one had taken the plaque down.

By the time I got back to my room it was almost dark, even though I'd splurged and taken a taxi. After the video, the thought of being trapped in the crowded, stinking subway, hurtling along through the city's bowels, through those tunnels where the sun never reaches, gave me a righteous fucking case of the heebie-jeebies and, what the hell, the Agency was picking up the tab. All those aspirin had left my stomach aching and sour, and hadn't done much of anything about the hangover, but there was an unopened pint waiting for me beneath the edge of the bed.

I was almost asleep when Sarah called.

Here's a better quote. I've been carrying it around with me for the last few years, in my head and on a scrap of paper. It showed up in my email one day, sent by some anonymous someone or another from an account that turned out to be bogus. Scrubbers get a lot of anonymous email. Tips, rumors, bullshit, hearsay, wicked little traps set by the Agency, confessions, nightmares, curses, you name it and it comes rolling our way, and after a while you don't even bother to wonder who sent the shit. But this one, this one kept me awake a few nights:

"But what would a deep-sea fish learn even if a steel plate of a wrecked vessel above him should drop and bump him on the nose?

Our submergence in a sea of conventionality of almost impenetrable density.

Sometimes I'm a savage who has found something on the beach of his island. Sometimes I'm a deep-sea fish with a sore nose.

The greatest of mysteries:

Why don't they ever come here, or send here, openly?

Of course, there's nothing to that mystery if we don't take so seriously the notion—that we must be interesting. It's probably for moral reasons that they stay away—but even so, there must be some degraded ones among them."

It's that last bit that always sinks its teeth (or claws or whatever the fuck have you) into me and hangs on. Charles Hoyt Fort. *The Book of the Damned*. First published in 1919, a century and a half before IcePIC, and it occurs to me now that I shouldn't be any less disturbed by prescience than I am by irony. But there you go. Sometimes I'm a savage. Sometimes I'm a deep-sea fish. And my life is become the sum of countless degradations.

"You're not going down there alone," Sarah said, telling, not asking, because, like I already noted, Sarah stopped being the kind of girl who asks questions when she signed on with the Agency for life plus whatever else they could milk her biomeched cadaver for. I didn't reply immediately, lay there a minute or three, rubbing my eyes, waiting for the headache to start in on me again, listening to the faint, insistent crackle from the phone. Manhattan's landlines were shit and roses that February, had been that way for years, ever since some Puerto Ricans in Brooklyn had popped a homemade micro-EMP rig to celebrate the Fourth of July. I wondered why Sarah hadn't called me on my thumbline while I looked about for the scotch. Turned out I was lying on the empty bottle, and I rolled over, wishing I'd never been born. I held the phone cradled between my left shoulder and my cheek and stared at the darkness outside the window of my hotel room.

"Do you even know what time it is?" I asked her.

"Templeton said you were talking about going out to Roosevelt. He said you might have gone already."

"I didn't say dick to Templeton about Roosevelt," I said, which was the truth—I hadn't—but also entirely beside the point. It was John Templeton's prerogative to stay a few steps ahead of his employees, especially when those employees were scrubbers, especially freebie scrubbers on the juice. I tossed the empty bottle at a cockroach on the wall across the room. The bottle didn't break, but squashed the roach and left a satisfying dent in the drywall.

"You know Agency protocol for dealing with terrorists."

"They went and stuck something in your head so you don't *have* to sleep anymore, is that it?"

"You can't go to the island alone," she said. "I'm sending a couple of plain-clothes men over. They'll be at your hotel by six a.m., at the latest."

"Yeah, and I'll be fucking asleep at six," I mumbled, more interested in watching the roaches that had emerged to feed on the remains of the one I'd nailed than arguing with her.

"We can't risk losing you, Mr. Paine. It's too late to call in someone else if anything happens. You know that as well as I do."

"Do I?"

"You're a drunk, not an idiot."

"Look, Sarah, if I start scutzing around out there with two of Temp's goons in tow, I'll be lucky if I *find* a fucking stitch, much less get it to talk to me."

"They're all animals," Sarah said, meaning the stitches and meatdolls and genetic changelings that had claimed Roosevelt Island a decade or so back. There was more than a hint of loathing in her voice. "It makes me sick, just thinking about them."

"Did you ever stop to consider they probably feel the same way about you?"

"No," Sarah said coldly, firmly, one-hundred percent shitsure of herself. "I never have."

"If those fuckers knock on my door at six o'clock, I swear to god, Sarah, I'll shoot them."

"I'll tell them to wait for you in the lobby."

"That's real damn thoughtful of you."

There was another static-littered moment of silence then, and I closed my eyes tight. The headache was back and had brought along a few friends for the party. My thoughts were starting to bleed together, and I wondered if I'd vomit before or after Sarah finally let me off the phone. I wondered if cyborgs vomited. I wondered exactly what all those agents in the black Chevy van had seen on their consoles and face screens when I'd walked over and touched a corner of the bed in the apartment on Columbus Avenue.

"I'm going to hang up now, Sarah. I'm going back to sleep."

"You're sober."

"As a judge," I whispered and glanced back at the window, trying to think about anything at all except throwing up. There were bright lights moving across the sky above the river, red and green and white, turning clockwise; one of the big military copters, an old Phoenix 6-98 or one of the newer Japanese whirlybirds, making its circuit around the Rotten Apple.

"You're still a lousy liar," she said.

"I'll have to try harder."

"Don't fuck this up, Mr. Paine. You're a valued asset. The Agency would like to see you remain that way."

"I'm going back to sleep," I said again, disregarding the not-so-subtle threat tucked between her words; it wasn't anything I didn't already know. "And I meant what I said about shooting those assholes. Don't think I didn't. Anyone knocks on this door before eight sharp, and that's all she wrote."

"They'll be waiting in the lobby when you're ready."

"Goodnight, Sarah."

"Goodnight, Mr. Paine," she replied, and a second or two later there was only the ragged dial tone howling in my ear. The lights outside the window were gone, the copter probably all the way to Harlem by now. I almost made it to the toilet before I was sick.

If I didn't keep getting the feeling that there's someone standing behind me, someone looking over my shoulder as I write this, I'd say more about the dreams. The dreams are always there, tugging at me, insistent, selfish, wanting to be spilled out into the wide, wide world where everyone and his brother can get a good long gander at them. They're not content anymore with the space *inside* my skull. My skull is a prison for dreams, an enclosed and infinite prison space where the arrows on the number line point towards each other, infinitely converging but never, ever, ever meeting and so infinite all the same. But I *do* keep getting that feeling, and there's still the matter of the thing in the apartment.

The thing on the bed.

The thing that the cop who'd been in Damascus after the Israelis' 40-megaton fireworks show died for.

My thirteenth and final contact.

After I was finished with the makeshift airlock at the door, one of Templeton's field medics, safe and snug inside a blue hazmat suit, led me through the brightly-lit apartment. I held one hand cupped over my nose and mouth, but the thick clouds of neon yellow disinfectant seeped easily between my fingers, gagging me. My eyes burned and watered, making it even more difficult to see. I've always thought that shit smelled like licorice, but it seems to smell like different things to different people. Sarah used to say it reminded her of burning tires. I used to know a guy who said it smelled like carnations.

"It's in the bedroom," the medic said, his voice flat and tinny through the suit's audio. "It doesn't seem to have spread to any of the other rooms. How was the jump from Los Angeles, sir?"

I didn't answer him, too ripped on adrenaline for small talk and pleasantries, and he didn't really seem to care, my silence just another part of the routine. I took shallow breaths and followed the medic through the yellow fog, which was growing much thicker as we approached ground zero. The disinfectant was originally manufactured by Dow for domestic bioterrorism clean-up, but the Agency's clever boys and girls had added a pinch of this, a dash of that, and it always seemed to do the job. We passed a kitchenette, beer cans and dirty dishes and an open box of corn flakes sitting on the counter, then turned left into a short hallway leading past a bathroom too small for a rat to take a piss in, past a framed photograph of a lighthouse on a rocky shore (the bits we remember, the bits we forget), to the bedroom. Templeton was there, of course, decked out in his orange hazmat threads, one hand resting confidently on the butt of the big Beretta Pulse 38A on his hip, and he pointed at me and then pointed at the bed.

Sometimes I'm a deep-sea fish.

Sometimes I'm a savage.

"We're still running MRS and backtrace on these two," Templeton said, pointing at the bed again, "but I'm pretty sure the crit's a local." His gray eyes peered warily out at me, the lights inside his hood shining bright so I had no trouble at all seeing his face through the haze.

"I figure one of them picked it up from an untagged mobile, probably the woman there, and it's been hitching dormant for the last few weeks. We're guessing the trigger was viral. She might have caught a cold. Corona's always a good catalyst."

I took a deep breath and coughed. Then I gagged again and stared up at the ceiling for a moment.

"Come on, Deet. I need you frosty on this one. You're not drunk, are you? Fennimore said-"

"I'm not drunk," I replied, and I wasn't, not yet. I hadn't had a drink in almost six months, but, hey, the *good* news was, the drought was almost over.

"That's great," Templeton said. "That's real damn great. That's exactly what I wanted to hear."

I looked back at the bed.

"So, when you gonna tell me what's so goddamn special about this one?" I asked. "The way Sarah sounded, I figured you'd already lost a whole building."

"What's so goddamn special about them, Deet, is that they're still conscious, both of them. Initial EEGs are coming up pretty solid. Clean alpha, beta, and delta. The theta's are weakening, but the brain guys say the waves are still synchronous enough to call coherent."

Temp kept talking, but I tuned him out and forced myself to take a long, hard look at the bed.

Sometimes I'm a deep-sea fish.

The woman's left eye was still intact, open very wide and wet with tears, her blue iris bright as Christmas Day, and I realized she was watching me.

"It's pure," Templeton said, leaning closer to the bed, "more than ninety-percent proximal to the Lælaps strain. Beats the fuck outta me why their brains aren't soup by now."

"I'm going to need a needle," I muttered, speaking automatically, some part of me still there to walk the walk and talk the talk, some part of me getting ready to take the plunge, because the only way out of this hole was straight ahead. A very small, insensate part of me not lost in that pleading blue eye. "Twelve and a half max, okay, and not that fife-and-drum Australian shit you gave me in Boston. I don't want to feel *anything* in there but the critter, you understand?"

"Sure," Templeton said, smiling like a ferret.

"I mean it. Whatever's going through their heads right now, I don't want to hear it, Temp. Not so much as a peep, not even a fucking whisper."

"Hey, you're calling the shots, Deet."

"Bullshit," I said. "Don't suck my dick, just get me the needle."

He motioned to a medic, and in a few more minutes the drugs were singing me towards that spiraling ebony pipeline, the Scrubber's Road, Persephone's Staircase, the Big Drop, the White Bull, whatever you want to call it, it's all the same to me. I was beginning to sweat and trying to make it through the procedure checklist one last time. Templeton patted me on the back, the way he always did when I was standing there on the brink. I said a silent prayer to anything that might be listening that one day it'd be his carcass rotting away at the center of the Agency's invisible clockwork circus. And then I kneeled down at the edge of the bed and got to work.

Sarah sent the goons over, just like she'd said she would, but I ducked out the back and, luckily, she hadn't seen fit to have any of Temp's people watching all the hotel's exits. Maybe she couldn't pull that many warm bodies off the main gig down on Columbus. Maybe Temp had bigger things on his mind. I caught a cash-and-ride taxi that took me all the way to the ruins along York Avenue. The Vietnamese driver hadn't wanted to get any closer to the Queensboro Bridge than Third, but I slipped him five hundred and he found a little more courage somewhere. He dropped me at the corner of Second and East Sixty-First Street, crossed himself twice, and drove away, bouncing recklessly over the trash and disintegrating blacktop. I watched him go, feeling more alone than I'd expected. Overhead, the Manhattan sky was the color of buttermilk and mud, and I wished briefly, pointlessly, that I'd brought a gun. The 9 mm Samson-L4 Enforcer I'd bought in a Hollywood pawnshop almost four years before was back at the hotel, hidden in a locked compartment of my suitcase. But I knew it'd be a whole lot worse to be picked up crossing the barricades without a pass if I were carrying an unregistered weapon, one more big red blinking excuse for the MPs to play a few rounds of Punch and Judy with my face while they waited for my papers and my story about the Agency to check out.

I started walking north, the gray-blue snow crunching loudly beneath my boots, the collar of my coat turned up against the wind whistling raw between the empty, burned-out buildings. I'd heard security was running slack around the Sixty-Third Street entrance. I might get lucky. It had happened before.

"Yes, but what exactly did you think you'd find on the island?" Buddhadev Krishnamurthy asked when he interviewed me for his second book on technoshamanism and the Roosevelt parahumanists, the one that won him a Pulitzer.

"Missing pieces, maybe," I replied. "I was just following my nose. The Miyake girl turned up during the contact."

"But going to the island alone, wasn't that rather above and beyond? I mean, if you hated Templeton and the Agency so much, why stick your neck out like that?"

"Old habits," I said, sipping at my tequila and trying hard to remember how long it had taken me to find a way past the guards and up onto the bridge. "Old habits and bad dreams," I added, and then, "But I never said I was doing it for the Agency." I knew I was telling him more than I'd intended. Not that it mattered. None of my interview made it past the censors and into print.

I kept to the center lanes, except for a couple of times when rusted and fire-blackened tangles of wrecked automobiles and police riot-rollers forced me to the edges of the bridge. The West Channel glimmered dark and iridescent beneath the late February clouds, a million shifting colors dancing lazily across the oily surface of the river. The wind shrieked through the cantilever spans, like angry sirens announcing my trespass to anyone who would listen. I kept waiting for the sound of helicopter rotors or a foot patrol on its way back from Queens, for some sharpshooter's bullet to drop me dead in my tracks. Maybe it was wishful thinking.

Halfway across I found the access stairs leading down to the island, right where my contact in Street and Sanitation had said they would be. I checked my watch. It was five minutes until noon.

"Will you tell me about the dreams, Mr. Paine?" Krishnamurthy asked, after he'd ordered me another beer and another shot of tequila. His voice was like silk and cream, the sort of voice that seduced, that tricked you into lowering your defenses just long enough for him to get a good peek at all the nasty nooks and crannies. "I hear lots of scrubbers had trouble with nightmares back then, before the new neural-drag sieves were available. The suicide rate's dropped almost 50-percent since they became standard issue. Did you know that, Mr. Paine?"

"No," I told him. "Guess I missed the memo. I'm kind of outside the flow these days."

"You're a lucky man," he said. "You should count your blessings. At least you made it out in one piece. At least you made it out sane."

I think I told him to fuck off then. I know I didn't tell him about the dreams.

"What do you see down there, Deet? The sensors are getting a little hinky on me," Sarah said and, in the dreams, back when, in the day, before the tweaker's silver chip, I took another clumsy step towards the edge of the chasm created by hot water welling up from the deep-sea vents along the Great Charon Ridge. A white plume of salty steam rose high into the thin Europan atmosphere, blotting out the western horizon, boiling off into the indifferent blackness of space. I knew I didn't want to look over the edge again. I'd been there enough times already, and it was always the same, and I reminded myself that no one had ever walked on Europa, no one human, and it was only a dream. Shit. Listen to me. *Only* a dream. Now, there's a contradiction to live by.

"Am I coming through?" Sarah asked. "Can you hear me?"

I didn't answer her. My mouth was too dry to speak, bone dry from fear and doubt and the desiccated air circulating through the helmet of my EMU suit.

"I need you to acknowledge, Deet. Can you hear me?"

The mouth of Sakpata, the plague gate, yawning toothless and insatiable before me, almost nine kilometers from one side to the other, more than five miles from the edge of the hole down to the water. I was standing near the center of the vast field of cryovolcanic lenticulae first photographed by the Galileo probe in 1998, on its fifteenth trip around Jupiter. Convection currents had pushed the crust into gigantic pressure domes that finally cracked and collapsed under their own weight, exposing the ocean below. I took another step, almost slipping on the ice, and wondered how far I was from the spot where IcePIC had made landfall.

"Deet, do you copy?"

"Do you believe in sin, Deet?"

Nor shapes of men nor beasts we ken—
The ice was all between.

Sarah sets her coffee cup down and watches me from the other side of our apartment on Cahuenga. Her eyes are still her eyes, full of impatience and secrets. She reaches for a cigarette, and I wish this part weren't a dream, that I could go back to *here* and start again. This sunny LA morning, Sarah wearing nothing but her bra and panties, and me still curled up in the warm spot she left in the sheets. Go back and change the words. Change every goddamn day that's come between now and then.

"They want my decision by tomorrow morning," she says and lights her cigarette. The smoke hangs like a caul about her face.

"Tell them you need more time," I reply. "Tell them you have to think about it."

"This is the fucking Agency," she says and shakes her head. "You don't ask them for more time. You don't ask them shit."

"I don't know what you want me to say, Sarah."

"It's everything I've always wanted," she says and flicks ash into an empty soft drink can.

Are those her ribs through which the Sun
Did peer, as through a grate?

I took another step nearer the chasm and wished that this would end and I would wake up. If I could wake up, I wouldn't have to see. If I could wake up, there'd be a bottle of scotch or bourbon or tequila waiting for me, a drink of something to take the edge off the dryness in my mouth. The sun was rising behind me, a distant, pale thing lost among the stars, and the commlink buzzed and crackled in my ears.

"If it's what you want, take it," I say, the same thing I always say, the same words I can never take back. "I'm not going to stand in your way." I could tell it was the last thing that Sarah wanted to hear. The End. The curtain falls and everyone takes a bow. The next day, Wednesday, I'll drive her to LAX-1, and she'll take the 4:15 jump to D.C.

We are more alone than ever.

Ronnie used her own blood to write those six words on the wall of her room at La Casa, the night she killed herself.

My boots left no trace whatsoever on the slick, blue-white ice. A few more steps and I was finally standing at the edge, walking cautiously onto the wide shelf formed by an angular chaos block jutting a few meters out over the pit. The constant steam had long since worn the edges of the block smooth. Eventually, this block would melt free, undercut by ages of heat and water vapor, and pitch into the churning abyss far below. I took a deep breath of the dry, stale air inside my helmet and peered into the throat of Sakpata.

"Tell me, what the hell did we expect to find out there, Deet?" Ronnie asked me. "What did we think it would be? Little gray men with the answers to all the mysteries of the universe, free for the asking? A few benign extremophiles clinging stubbornly to the bottom of an otherwise lifeless sea? I can't *remember* anymore. I try, but I can't. I lie awake at night trying to remember."

"I don't think it much matters," I told her, and she started crying again.

"It was waiting for us, Deet," she sobbed. "It was waiting for us all along, a million fucking years alone out there in the dark. It knew we'd come, sooner or later."

Sarah was standing on the ice behind me, naked, the wind tearing at her plastic skin.

"Why do you keep coming here?" she asked. "What do you think you'll find?"

"Why do you keep following me?"

"You turned off your comms. I wasn't getting a signal. You didn't leave me much choice."

I turned to face her, turning my back on the hole, but the wind had already pulled her apart and scattered the pieces across the plain.

We are more alone than ever.

And then I'm in the pipe, slipping along the Scrubber's Road, no friction, no resistance, rushing by high above the frozen moon, waiting for that blinding, twinkling moment of perfect agony when my mind brushes up against that other mind. That instant when it tries to hide, tries to withdraw, and I dig in and hang on and drag it screaming into the light. I hear the whir of unseen machineries as the techs on the outside try to keep up with me, with it.

I stand alone at the edge of Sakpata's mouth, where no man has ever stood, at the foot of the bed on Columbus, in the airport lobby saying goodbye to Sarah. I have all my cameras, my instruments, because I'll need all that later on, when the spin is over and I'm drunk and there's nothing left but the footwork.

When I have nothing left to do but track down the carrier and put a bullet or two in his or her or its head.

Cut the cord. Tie off the loose ends.

"Do you believe in sin, Deet?"

Instead of the cross, the Albatross...

"It's only a question. Stop trying to make it anything more than that."

"Do you copy?" Sarah asks again. "Global can't get a fix on you." I take another step closer to the hole, and it slips a few feet farther away from me. The sky is steam and stars and infinite night.

I followed East Road north to Main Street, walking as quickly as the snow and black ice and wrecks littering the way would allow. I passed through decaying canyons of brick and steel, broken windows and gray concrete, the tattered ruins of the mess left after the Feds gave Roosevelt Island up for lost, built their high barricades and washed their righteous hands of the place. I kept my eyes on the road at my feet, but I could feel them watching me, following me, asking each other if this one was trouble or just some fool out looking for his funeral. I might have been either. I still wasn't sure myself. There were tracks in the snow and frozen mud, here and there, some of them more human than others.

Near the wild place that had once been Blackwell Park, I heard something call out across the island. It was a lonely, frightened sound, and I walked a little faster.

I wondered if Sarah would try to send an extraction team in after me, if she was in deep sharn with Templeton and the boys for letting me scoot. I wondered if maybe Temp was already counting me among the dead and kicking himself for not putting me under surveillance, trying to figure out how the hell he was going to lay it all out for the bastards in Washington. It took me the better part of an hour to reach the northern tip of the island and the charred and crumbling corpse of Coler-Goldwater Hospital. The ragtag militia of genetic anarchists who had converged on Manhattan in the autumn of '69, taking orders from a schizo ex-movie star who called herself Circe Nineteen, had claimed the old hospital as their headquarters. When the army decided to start shelling, Coler had taken the worst of the mortars. Circe Nineteen had been killed by a sniper, but there'd been plenty of freaks on hand to fill her shoes, so to speak.

Beneath the sleeting February sky, the hospital looked as dead as the day after Armageddon. I tried not to think about the spooch, all the things I'd seen and heard the day before, the things I'd felt, the desperate stream of threats and promises and prayers the crit had spewed at me when I'd finally come to the end of the shimmering aether pipeline and we'd started the dance.

Inside, the hospital stunk like a zoo, a dying, forgotten zoo, but at least I was out of the wind. My face and hands had gone numb. How would the Agency feel about a scrubber without his fingers? Would they toss me on the scrap heap, or would they just give me a shiny new set, made in Osaka, better than the originals? Maybe work a little of the biomech magic they'd worked on Sarah? I followed a long ground-floor hallway past doors and doorways without doors, pitch dark rooms and chiaroscuro rooms ruled by the disorienting interplay of shadow and light, until I came to a row of elevators. All the doors had been jammed more or less open at some point, exposing shafts filled with dust and gears and rusted cables. I stood there a while, as my fingers and lips began to tingle, the slow pins-and-needles thaw, and listened to the building whispering around me.

"They're all animals," Sarah had sneered the day before. But they weren't, of course, no more than she was truly a machine. I knew Sarah was bright enough to see the truth, even before they'd squeezed all that hardware into her skull. Even if she could never admit it to herself or anyone else. The cyborgs and H+ brigade were merely opposing poles in the same rebellion against the flesh—black pawn, white pawn—north and south on the same twisted post-evolutionary road. Not that it made much difference to me. It sill doesn't. But standing there, my breath fogging and the feeling slowly returning to my hands, her arrogance was pissing me off more than usual. Near as I could tell, the biggest difference between Sarah and whatever was waiting for me in the bombed-out hospital that afternoon—maybe the only difference that actually mattered—was that the men and women in power had found a use for her kind, while the stitches and changelings had never been anything to them but a nuisance. It might have gone a different way. It might yet.

There was a stairwell near the elevators, and I climbed it to the third floor. I hadn't thought to bring a flashlight with me, so I stayed close to the wall, feeling my way through the gloom, stumbling more than once when my feet encountered chunks of rubble that had fallen from somewhere overhead.

On the third floor, the child was waiting for me.

"What do you want here?" he barked and blinked at me with the golden eyes of a predatory bird. He was naked, his skin hidden beneath a coat of fine yellow-brown fur.

"Who are you?" I asked him.

"The manticore said you were coming. She saw you on the bridge. What do you want?"

"I'm looking for a girl named Jet."

The child laughed, a strange, hitching laugh and rolled his eyes. He leaned forward, staring at me intently, expectantly, and the vertical pupils of those big golden eyes dilated slightly.

"Ain't no *girls* here, Mister," he chuckled. "Not anymore. You skizzled or what?"

"Is there anyone here named Jet? I've come a long way to talk to her."

"You got a gun, maybe?" he asked. "You got a knife?"

"No," I said. "I don't. I just want to talk."

"You come out to Stitchtown without a gun *or* a knife? Then you must have some bangers, Mister. You must have whennymegs big as my fist," and he held up one clenched fist so I could see exactly what he meant. "Or you don't want to live so much longer, maybe."

"Maybe," I replied.

"Meat's scarce this time of year," the boy chuckled and then licked his thin ebony lips.

Down at the other end of the hallway, something growled softly, and the boy glanced over his shoulder, then back up at me. He was smiling, a hard smile that was neither cruel nor kind, revealing the sharp tips of his long canines and incisors. He looked disappointed.

"All in good time," he said and took my hand. "All in good time," and I let him lead me towards the eager shadows crouched at the other end of the hallway.

Near the end of his book, Emmanuel Weatherby-Jones writes, "The calamities following, and following from, the return of the IcePIC probe may stand as mankind's gravest defeat. For long millennia, we had asked ourselves if we were alone in the cosmos. Indeed, that question has surely formed much of the fundamental matter of the world's religions. But when finally answered, once and for all, we were forced to accept that there had been greater comfort in our former, vanished ignorance."

We are more alone than ever. Ronnie got that part right.

When I'd backed out of the contact and the techs had a solid lockdown on the critter's signal, when the containment waves were pinging crystal mad off the putrescent walls of the bedroom on Columbus and one of the medics had administered a stimulant to clear my head and bring me the rest of the way home, I sat down on the floor and cried.

Nothing unusual about that. I've cried almost every single time. At least I didn't puke.

"Good job," Templeton said and rested a heavy gloved hand on my shoulder.

"Fuck you. I could hear them. I could hear both of them, you asshole."

"We did what we could, Deet. I couldn't have you so tanked on morphine you'd end up flat lining."

"Oh my god. Oh Jesus god," I sobbed like an old woman, gasping, my heart racing itself round smaller and smaller circles, fried to a crisp on the big syringe full of synthetadrine the medic had pumped into my left arm. "Kill it, Temp. You kill it right this fucking instant."

"We have to stick to protocol," he said calmly, staring down at the writhing mass of bone and meat and protoplasm on the bed. A blood-red tendril slithered from the place where the man's mouth had been and began burrowing urgently into the sagging mattress. "Just as soon as we have you debriefed and we're sure stasis is holding, then we'll terminate life signs."

"Fuck it," I said and reached for his Beretta, tearing the pistol from the velcro straps of the holster with enough force that Temp almost fell over on top of me. I shoved him aside and aimed at the thing on the bed.

"Deet, don't you even fucking *think* about pulling that trigger!"

"You can go straight to Hell," I whispered, to Templeton, to the whole goddamn Agency, to the spooch and that single hurting blue eye still watching me. I squeezed the trigger, emptying the whole clip into what little was left of the man and woman's swollen skulls, hoping it would be enough.

Then someone grabbed for the gun, and I let them take it from me.

"You stupid motherfucker," Temp growled. "You goddamn, stupid bastard. As soon as this job is finished, you are *out*. Do you fucking understand me, Deet? You are *history*!"

"Yeah," I replied and sat back down on the floor. In the silence left after the roar of the gun, the containment waves pinged, and my ears rang, and the yellow fog settled over me like a shroud.

At least, that's the way I like to pretend it all went down. Late at night, when I can't sleep, when the pills and booze aren't enough, I like to imagine there was one moment in my wasted, chicken-shit life when I did what I should have done.

Whatever really happened, I'm sure someone's already written it down somewhere. I don't have to do it again.

In the cluttered little room at the end of the third-floor hall-way, the woman with a cat's face and nervous, twitching ears sat near a hole that had been a window before the mortars. There was no light but the dim winter sun. The boy sat at her feet and never took his eyes off me. The woman—if she had a name, I never learned it—only looked at me once, when I first entered the room. The fire in her eyes made short work of whatever resolve I had left, and I was glad when she turned back to the hole in the wall and stared north across the river towards the Astoria refineries.

She told me the girl had left a week earlier. She didn't have any idea where Jet Miyake might have gone.

"She brings food and medicine, sometimes," the woman said, confirming what I'd already suspected. Back then, there were a lot of people willing to risk prison or death to get supplies to Roosevelt Island. Maybe there still are. I couldn't say.

"I'm sorry to hear about her parents," she said.

"It was quick," I lied. "They didn't suffer."

"You smell like death, Mr. Paine," the woman said, flaring her nostrils slightly. The boy at her feet laughed and hugged himself, rocking from side to side. "I think it follows you. I believe you herald death."

"Yeah, I think the same thing myself sometimes," I replied.

"You hunt the aliens?" she purred.

"That's one way of looking at it."

"There's a certain irony, don't you think? Our world was dying. We poisoned *our* world and then went looking for life somewhere else. Do you think we found what we were looking for, Mr. Paine?"

"No," I told her. "I don't think we ever will."

"Go back to the city, Mr. Paine. Go now. You won't be safe after sunset. Some of us are starving. Some of our children are starving."

I thanked her and left the room. The boy followed me as far as the stairs, then he stopped and sat chuckling to himself, his laughter echoing through the stairwell, as I moved slowly, step by blind step, through the uncertain darkness. I retraced my path to the street, following Main to East, past the wild places, through the canyons, and didn't look back until I was standing on the bridge again.

I found Jet Miyake in Chinatown two days later, hiding out in the basement of the Buddhist Society of Wonderful Enlightenment on Madison Street. The Agency had files on a priest there, demonstrating a history of pro-stitch sentiment. Jet Miyake ran, because they always run if they can, and I chased her, down Mechanics Alley, across Henry, and finally caught up with her in a fish market on East Broadway, beneath the old Manhattan Bridge. She tried to lose me in the maze of kiosks, the glistening mounds of octopus and squid, eel and tuna and cod laid out on mountains of crushed ice. She headed for a back door and almost made it, but slipped on the wet concrete floor and went sprawling ass over tits into a big display of dried soba and canned chicken broth. I don't actually remember all those details, just the girl and the stink of fish, the clatter of the cans on the cement, the angry, frightened shouts from the merchants and customers. But the details, the octopus and soba noodles, I don't know. I think I'm trying to forget this isn't fiction, that it happened, that I'm not making it up as I go along.

Sometimes.

Sometimes I'm a savage.

I held the muzzle of my pistol to her right temple while I ran the scan. She gritted her teeth and stared silently up at me. The machine read her dirty as the gray New York snow, though I didn't need the blinking red light on the genetigraph to tell me that. She was hurting, the way only long-term carriers can hurt. I could see it in her eyes, in the sweat streaming down her face, in the faintly bluish tinge of her lips. She'd probably been contaminated for months. I knew it'd be a miracle if she'd infected no one but her parents. I showed her the display screen on the genetigraph and told her what it meant, and I told her what I had to do next.

"You can't stop it, you know," she said, smiling a bitter, sickly smile. "No matter how many people you kill, it's too late. It's been too late from the start."

"I'm sorry," I said, whether I actually was or not, and squeezed the trigger. The 9mm boomed like thunder in a bottle, and suddenly she wasn't my problem anymore. Suddenly she was just another carcass for the sweepers.

I have become an unreliable narrator. Maybe I've been an unreliable narrator all along. Just like I've been a coward and a hypocrite all along. The things we would rather remember, the things we choose to forget. As the old saying goes, it's only a movie.

I didn't kill Jet Miyake.

"You can't stop it, you know," she said. That part's the truth. "No matter how many people you kill, it's too late. It's been too late from the start."

"I'm sorry," I said.

"We brought it here. We invited it in, and it likes what it sees. It means to stay." She did smile, but it was a satisfied, secret smile. I stepped back and lowered the muzzle of the gun. The bore had left a slight circular impression on her skin.

"Please step aside, Mr. Paine," Sarah said, and when I turned around she was standing just a few feet behind me, pointing a ridiculously small carbon-black Glock at the girl. Sarah fired twice and waited until the body stopped convulsing, then put a third bullet in Jet Miyake's head, just to be sure. Sarah had always been thorough.

"Templeton thought you might get cold feet," she said and stepped past me, kneeling to inspect the body. "You know this means that you'll probably be suspended."

"She was right, wasn't she?" I muttered. "Sooner or later, we're going to lose this thing," and for a moment I considered putting a few rounds into Sarah's skull, pulling the trigger and spraying brains and blood and silicon across the floor of the fish market. It might have been a mercy killing. But I suppose I didn't love her quite as much as I'd always thought. Besides, the Agency would have probably just picked up the pieces and stuck her back together again.

"One day at a time, Mr. Paine," she said. "That's the only way to stay sane. One day at a time."

"No past, no future."

"If that's the way you want to look at it."

She stood up and held out a hand. I popped the clip from my pistol and gave her the gun and the ammo. I removed the genetigraph from my belt, and she took that, too.

"We'll send someone to the hotel for the rest of your equipment. Please have everything in order. You have your ticket back to Los Angeles."

"Yes," I said. "I have my ticket back to Los Angeles."

"You lasted a lot longer than I thought you would," she said.

And I left her there, standing over the girl's body, calling in the kill, ordering the sweeper crew. The next day I flew back to LA and found a bar where I was reasonably sure no one would recognize me. I started with tequila, moved on to scotch, and woke up two days later, facedown in the sand at Malibu, sick as a dog. The sun was setting, brewing a firestorm on the horizon, and I watched the stars come out above the sea. A meteor streaked across the sky and was gone. It only took me a moment to find Jupiter, Lord of the Heavens, Gatherer of Clouds, hardly more than a bright pin-prick near the moon.

Faces in Revolving Souls

The woman named Sylvia, who might as well still be a child, is waiting for the elevator that will carry her from the twenty-third floor of the hotel—down, down, down like a sinking stone—to the lobby and convention registration area. She isn't alone in the hallway, though she wishes that she were. There are several others waiting to sink with her—a murmuring, laughing handful of stitches and meat dolls busy showing off the fact that they're not new at this, that they belong here, busy making sure that Sylvia knows they can see just exactly how birth-blank she is. Not quite a virgin, no, but the next worst thing, and all that pink skin to give her away, the pink skin and the silver-blue silk dress with its sparkling mandarin collar, the black espadrilles on her feet. The others are all naked, for the most part, and Sylvia keeps her head down, her eyes trained on the toes of her shoes, because the sight of them reflected in the polished elevator doors makes her heart race and her mouth go dry.

No one knows I'm here, she thinks again, relishing the simple nervous delight she feels whenever she imagines her mother or sisters or someone at work discovering that she lied to them all about going to Mexico, and where she's gone, instead. She knows that if they knew, if they ever found out, they'd want explanations. And that if she ever tried to explain, they'd do their best to have her locked away, or worse. There's still a multitude of psychiatrists who consider polymorphy a sickness, and politicians who consider it a crime, and priests who consider it blasphemy.

A bell hidden somewhere in the wall rings, and the elevator doors slide silently open. Sylvia steps quickly into the empty elevator, and the others follow her—the woman who is mostly a leopard, the fat man with thick brown fur and eyes like a raven, the pretty teenage girl with stubby antlers and skin the color of ripe cranberries—all of them filing in, one by one, like the passengers of some lunatic Noah's ark. Sylvia stands all the way at the rear, her back turned to them, and stares out through the transparent wall as the elevator falls and the first floor of the hotel swiftly rises up to meet her. It only stops once on the way down, at the fourth floor, and she doesn't turn to see who or what gets on. It's much too warm inside the elevator and the air smells like sweat and musk and someone's lavender-scented perfume.

"Yes, of course," the leopard says to the antlered girl with cranberry skin. "But this will be the first time I've ever seen her in person." The leopard lisps and slurs when she speaks, human vocal cords struggling with a rough feline tongue, with a mouth that has been rebuilt for purposes other than talking.

"First time, I saw her at Berkeley," the antlered girl replies. "And then again at Chimera last year."

"You were at Chimera last year?" someone asks, sounding surprised, and maybe even skeptical; Sylvia thinks it must be whoever got on at the fourth floor, because she hasn't heard this sexless voice before. "I made it down for the last two days. You were there?"

"Yeah, I was there," the girl says. "But you probably wouldn't remember me. That was back before my dermals started to show."

"And *all* the girls are growing antlers these days," the leopard lisps, and everyone laughs, all of them except Sylvia. None of them sound precisely human anymore, and their strange, bestial laughter is almost enough to make Sylvia wish that she'd stayed home, almost enough to convince her that she's in over her head, drowning, and maybe she isn't ready for this, after all.

Another secret bell rings, and the doors slide open again, releasing them into the brightly lit lobby. First in, so last out, and

Sylvia has to squeeze through the press of incoming bodies, the people who'd been waiting for the elevator. She says "Excuse me," and "Pardon me," and tries not to look anyone in the eye or notice the particulars of their chosen metamorphoses.

Fera is waiting for her, standing apart from the rest, standing with her long arms crossed; she smiles when she sees Sylvia, showing off her broad canines. There's so little left of Fera that anyone would bother calling human, and the sight of her—the mismatched, improbable beauty of her—always leaves Sylvia lost and fumbling for words. Fera is one of the old-timers, an elder changeling, one of the twenty-five signatories on the original Provisional Proposition for Parahuman Secession.

"I was afraid you might have missed your flight," she says, and Sylvia knows that what she really means is, *I was afraid you'd chickened out.* Fera's voice is not so slurred or difficult to understand as the leopard's. She's had almost a decade to learn the mechanics of her new mandibular and lingual musculature, years to adapt to her altered tongue and palate.

"I just needed to unpack," Sylvia tells her. "I can't stand leaving my suitcases packed."

"I have some friends in the bar who would like to meet you," Fera purrs. "I've been telling them about your work."

"Oh," Sylvia whispers, because she hadn't expected that and doesn't know what else to say.

"Don't worry, Syl. They know you're still a neophyte. They're not expecting a sphinx."

Sylvia nods her head and glances back towards the elevator. The doors have closed again, and there's only her reflection staring back at her. *I look terrified,* she thinks. *I look like someone who wants to run.*

"Did you forget something?" Fera asks, and takes a step towards Sylvia. The thick pads of her paws are silent on the carpet, but the many hundreds of long quills that sprout from her shoulders and back, from her arms and the sides of her face, rustle like dry autumn leaves.

"No," Sylvia says, not at all sure whether or not she's telling the truth.

"I know you're nervous. It's only natural."

"But I feel like such a fool," Sylvia replies, and then she laughs a laugh that has no humor in it at all, a sound almost as dry as the noise of Fera's quills.

"Hey, you should have seen me, back in the day. I was a god-damn basket case," and Fera takes both her hands, as Sylvia turns to face her again. "It's a long road, and sometimes the first steps are the most difficult."

Sylvia looks down at Fera's hands, her nails grown to sharp, retractable claws, her skin showing black as an oil spill where it isn't covered in short auburn fur. Though she still has thumbs, there are long dewclaws sprouting from her wrists. Sylvia knows how much those hands would scare most people, how they would horrify all the blanks still clinging to their illusions of inviolable, immutable humanity. But they make her feel safe, and she holds them tight and forces a smile for Fera.

"Well, we don't want to keep your friends waiting," Sylvia says. "It's bad enough, me showing up wearing all these damned clothes. I don't want them to think I'm rude in the bargain."

Fera laughs, a sound that's really more like barking, and she kisses Sylvia lightly on her left cheek. "You just try to relax, *mon enfant trouvé*. And trust me. They're absolutely gonna love—" but then someone interrupts her, another leopard, a pudgy boy cat clutching a tattered copy of *The Children of Artemis*, which Fera signs for him. And she listens patiently to the questions he asks, all of which could have been answered with a quick internet search. Sylvia pretends not to eavesdrop on an argument between one of the hotel staff and a woman with crocodile skin, and when the leopard boy finally stops talking, Fera leads Sylvia away from the crowded elevators towards one of the hotel's bars.

And this is before—before the flight from Detroit to LAX, before the taxi ride to the hotel in Burbank. This is before the bad dreams she had on the plane, before the girl with cranberry skin, before the elevator's controlled fall from the twenty-third floor of the Marriott. This is a night and an hour and a moment from a whole year before Fera Delacroix takes her hand and leads her out of the lobby to the bar where there are people waiting to meet her.

"What's *this*?" her mother asks in the same sour, accusatory tone she's wielded all of Sylvia's life. And Sylvia, who's just come home from work and has a migraine, stares at the scatter of magazines and pamphlets lying on the dining table in front of her, trying to make sense of the question and all the glossy, colorful paper. Trying to think through the pain and the sudden, sick fear coiled cold and tight in her gut.

"I asked you a question, Sylvia," her mother says. "What are you doing with this crap?"

And Sylvia opens her mouth to reply, but her tongue doesn't want to cooperate. Down on the street, she can hear the traffic, and the distant rumble of a skipjet somewhere far overhead, and the sleepy drone of the refrigerator from the next room.

"I want an answer," her mother says and taps the cover of an issue of *Genshift* with her right index finger.

"Where did you get those?" Sylvia asks finally, but her voice seems farther away than the skipjet's turbines. "You've been in my room again, haven't you?"

"This is my house, young lady, and I'm asking you the questions," her mother growls, growling like a pit bull, like something mean and hungry straining at its fraying leash. "What are you doing with all this sick shit?"

And the part of Sylvia's mind that knows how to lie, the part that keeps her secrets safe and has no problem saying whatever needs to be said, takes over. "It's one of my stories," she says, trying hard to sound indignant, instead of frightened. "It's all just research. I brought it home last week—"

"Bullshit. Since when does the network waste time with this kind of deviant crap?" her mother demands, and she taps the magazine again. On the cover, there's a nude woman with firm brown nipples and the gently curved, corkscrew horns of an impala.

"Just because you don't happen to approve of the changelings doesn't mean they aren't news," Sylvia tells her, and hastily begins gathering up all the pamphlets and magazines. "Do you have any idea how many people have had some sort of interspecific genetic modification over the last five years?"

"Are you a goddamn lesbian?" her mother asks, and Sylvia catches the smell of gin on her breath.

"What?"

"They're all a bunch of queers and perverts," her mother mumbles and then snatches one of the Fellowship of Parahuman Evolutionists pamphlets from Sylvia's hands. "If this is supposed to be work for the network, why'd you have to go and hide it all under your bed?"

"I wasn't *hiding* anything, mother, and this isn't any of your business," and Sylvia yanks the pamphlet back from her mother. "How many times have I asked you to stay out of my room?"

"It's *my* house, and—"

"That means I have no privacy?"

"No ma'am. Not if it means you bringing this smut into my house."

"Jesus, it's for *work*. You want to call Mr. Padgett right now and have him tell you the same damned thing?" And there, it's out before she thinks better of pushing the lie that far, pushing it as far as it'll go, and there's no taking it back again.

"I ought to do that, young lady. You bet. That's *exactly* what I ought to do."

"So do it, and leave me alone. You know the number."

"Don't you think I won't."

"I have work to do before dinner," Sylvia says, as calmly as she can manage, turning away from her mother, beginning to wonder if she'll make it upstairs before she throws up. "I have a headache, and I really don't need you yelling at me right now."

"Don't think that I *won't* call. I'm a Christian woman, and I don't want that filth under my roof, you understand me, Sylvia?"

She doesn't reply, because there's nothing left to be said, and the cold knot in her belly has started looking for a way out, the inevitable path of least resistance. She takes her briefcase and the magazines and heads for the hallway and the stairs leading away from her mother. *Just keep walking,* she thinks. *Whatever else she says, don't even turn around. Don't say anything else to her. Not another word. Don't give her the satisfaction—*

"I know all about those people," her mother mumbles. "They're *filth,* you understand? *All* of them. Every single, goddamned one."

And then Sylvia's on the stairs, and her footsteps on the varnished wood are louder than her mother's voice. She takes them two at a time, almost running to the top, and locks her bedroom door behind her. Sylvia hurls the stack of changeling literature to the floor in a violent flutter of pages, and the antelope girl's large, dark eyes gaze blamelessly back up at her. She sits down with her back against the door, not wanting to cry but crying anyway, crying because at least it's better than vomiting.

And later—after her first three treatments at the Lycaon Clinic in Chicago, after the flight to LA, after Fera Delacroix takes her hand and leads her into the murmur and half light of the hotel bar—she'll understand that *this* afternoon, this moment, was her turning point. She'll look back and see clearly that this is the day she knew what she would do, no matter how much it terrified her, and no matter what it would mean, in the end.

They sit in a corner of the crowded, noisy bar, two tables pulled together to make room for everyone, this perfect, unreal menagerie. Sylvia sits to the left of Fera, sipping at a watery Coke. Fera's already introduced her to them all, a heady mix of changeling minor royalty and fellow travelers, and Sylvia has been sitting quietly for the last fifteen minutes, listening to them talk, trying to memorize their names, trying not to stare.

"It's a damned dangerous precedent," the man sitting directly across from her says. He has the night-seeing eyes of a python, and he drums his long claws nervously against the top of the table. His name is Maxwell White, and he's a geneticist at Johns Hopkins. Her last year in college, Sylvia read his book, *Looking for Moreau: A Parahumanist Manifesto.* It's made the American Library Association's list of most frequently banned books seven years straight.

"What the hell," Fera says. "I figure, it's just fucking Nebraska—"

Maxwell White stops drumming his fingers and sighs, his long ears going flat against the sides of his skull. "Sure, this year it's just fucking Nebraska. But, the way things are headed, next year it's going to be Nebraska and Alabama and Utah and—"

"We can't afford to be elitists," says a woman with iridescent scales that shimmer faintly in the dim light. As she talks, the tip end of her blue forked tongue flicks across her lips; Sylvia can't recall her name, only that she was recently fired from Duke University. "Not anymore. That asshole De Vries and his army of zealots is getting more press than the war."

"Oh, come on. It's not *that* bad," Fera says and frowns.

"How bad does it have to be?" Maxwell White asks and starts drumming his claws again. "Where do you think this is going to stop? After these anti-crossbreeding laws are in place and people get used to the idea that it's acceptable to restrict who we can and can't marry, who we can fuck, how long do you think it's going to take before we start seeing laws preventing us from voting or owning property or—"

"Maybe that's what we get for signing a declaration of secession from the human race," Fera replies, and Maxwell White makes an angry snorting sound.

"Jesus Christ, Fera, sometimes I wonder which side you're on."

"All I'm saying is I'm not so sure we can realistically expect to have it both ways. We tell them we're not the same as them anymore. That, by choice, each of us will exist as our own separate species, and then we act surprised when they want to treat us like animals."

"De Vries has already started talking about concentration camps," a woman named Alex Singleton says; she glances apprehensively at Fera and then quickly back down at the napkin she's been folding and unfolding for the past ten minutes. Alex Singleton has the striped, blonde fur of a tiger-lion hybrid, and six perfectly formed breasts. "Are you still going to be talking like this when they start rounding us up and locking us in cages?" she asks, and unfolds the napkin again.

"That's never going to happen," Fera replies, and scowls at Alex Singleton. "I'm not saying there aren't a lot of scary people out there. Of course, there are. We've just given the bigots and xenophobes something new to hate, that's all. We knew there'd be a difficult adjustment period, didn't we?"

"You have the most sublime knack for understatement," Maxwell White laughs.

And then Fera turns to Sylvia and smiles, that smile so beautiful that it's enough to make her dizzy, to make her blush. "You're awfully quiet over here, Syl. What do you think of all this? You think we're all about to be rounded up and herded off to a zoo?"

"I'm afraid I've never been much for politics," Sylvia says, not meaning to whisper, but her voice is almost lost in the din of the bar. "I mean, I don't guess I've thought much about it."

"Of course, she hasn't," Alex Singleton mutters. "Look at her. She still wears clothes. She's pink as—"

"I think maybe what Alex is trying to say, in her own indelicate way," the woman with iridescent scales interrupts, "is that you're probably going to find the political ramifications of our little revolution will suddenly seem a lot more important to you, once you start showing."

"That's not at all what I was trying to say."

"Some of us forget they were ever blank," Fera says, glaring at Alex Singleton, and she stirs at her martini with an olive skewered on a tiny plastic cutlass.

The thin man sitting next to Maxwell White clears his throat and waves at Sylvia with a hand that's really more of a paw. "Fera tells us you're one of Collier's patients," he says, speaking very slowly, his lupine jaws and tongue struggling with the words. "He's a good man."

"I'm very happy with him," Sylvia replies, and takes another sip of her Coke.

"He did my second stage," the wolf man confides, and his black lips draw back in a snarl, exposing sharp yellow canines and incisors. It takes Sylvia a moment to realize that the man's smiling.

"So," Maxwell White says, leaning towards her, "what's *your* story, Sylvia?"

"Like Fera said, I'm a journalist, and I'm preparing to write a book on the history—"

"No, that's not what I'm asking you."

"I'm sorry. Then I guess I didn't understand the question."

"Apparently not."

"Max here is one-third complete bastard," Fera says and jabs an ebony thumb at Maxwell White. "It was a tricky bit of bioengineering, but the results are a wonder to behold." Half the people at the two tables laugh out loud, and Sylvia is beginning to wish that she'd stayed in her room, that she'd never let Fera Delacroix talk her into coming to Burbank in the first place.

"Is it some sort of secret, what you're hiding under that dress?" Maxwell White asks, and Sylvia shakes her head.

"No," she says. "It's not a secret. I mean—"

"Then what's the problem?"

"Back off just a little, Max," Fera says, and the man with python eyes nods his head and shrugs.

"He does this to everyone, almost," Alex Singleton says and begins to shred her napkin. "He did it to me."

"It's not a secret," Sylvia says again. "I just—"

"You don't have to tell anyone here anything you're not ready to tell them, Syl," Fera assures her and kisses her cheek. Fera Delacroix's breath smells like vodka and olives. "You *know* that."

"It's just that none of *us* are wearing masks," Maxwell White says. "You might have noticed that."

"Excuse me, please," Sylvia says, suddenly close to tears and her heart beating like the wings of a small and terrified bird trapped deep inside her chest. She stands up too fast, bumps the table hard with her right knee, and almost spills her drink.

"You're a son of a bitch," Fera growls at Maxwell White, and she bares her teeth. "I hope you know that."

"No, really, it's okay," Sylvia says, forcing an unconvincing smile. "I'm fine. I understand, and I'm fine. I just need some fresh air, that's all."

And then she leaves them all sitting there in the shadows, murmuring and laughing among themselves. Sylvia doesn't look back, concentrates, instead, on the sound of her espadrilles against the wide stone tiles, and she makes it almost all the way to the elevators before Fera catches up with her.

On the plane, somewhere high above the Rockies and streaking towards Los Angeles through clearing, night-bound skies, Sylvia drifts between the velvet and gravel folds of dream sleep. She dozed off with the volume setting on her tunejack pushed far enough towards MAX that the noise of the flight attendants and the other passengers and the skipjet's turbines wouldn't wake her. So, there's only Beethoven's 6th Symphony getting in from the outside, and the voices inside her head. She's always hated flying, and took two of the taxi-cab yellow Placidmil capsules her therapist prescribed after her first treatment gave her insomnia.

In the nightmare, she stands alone on the crumbling bank of a sluggish, muddy river washed red as blood by the setting sun. She doesn't know the name of the city rising up around her, and suspects that it has no name. Only dark and empty windows, skyscrapers like broken teeth, the ruins of bridges that long ago carried the city's vanished inhabitants from one side of the wide red river to the other.

The river is within us, the sea is all about us, and isn't that what Matthew Arnold wrote, or T. S. Eliot, or Maharshi Ramakrishna, or some other long dead man? Sylvia takes a step nearer the river, and a handful of earth tumbles into the water. The ripples spread out from the shore, until the current pulls them apart.

Behind her, something has begun to growl—a low and threatful sound, the sound of something that might tear her apart in an instant. She glances over her shoulder, but there's only the buckled, abandoned street behind her and then the entrance to an alleyway. It's already midnight in the alley, and she knows that the growling thing is waiting for her there, where it has always waited for her. She turns back to the river, because the thing in the alley is patient, and the swollen crimson sun is still clinging stubbornly to the western horizon.

And now she sees that it's not the sunset painting the river red, but the blood of the dead and dying creatures drowning in the rising waters. The river devours their integrity, wedding one to the other, flesh to flesh, bone to bone. In another moment, there's only a single strangling organism, though a thousand pairs of eyes stare back at her in agony and horror, and two thousand hearts bleed themselves dry through a million ruptured veins.

And the way up is the way down, the way forward is the way back.

Countless talons and fingers, flippers and fins, tear futilely at the mud and soft earth along the river's edge, but all are swept away. And when the sun has gone, Sylvia turns to face the alley, and the growling thing that is her life, and wakes to the full moon outside the skipjet's window.

"You can't expect more of them," Fera says, "Not more than you expect of the straights, not just because they're going through the same thing you are."

"None of us are going through the same thing," Sylvia replies, not caring whether or not Fera hears the bitterness in her voice. "We're all going through this alone. Every one of us is alone, just like White said in his book. Every one of us is a species of one."

"I think you expect too much," Fera says, and then the elevator has reached the twenty-third floor, and the hidden bell rings, and the doors slide silently open. Sylvia steps out into the hall.

"Please promise me you won't spend the whole weekend locked in your room," Fera says. "At least come back down for Circe Seventeen's panel at eight, and—"

"Yeah," Sylvia says as the doors slide shut again. "Sure. I'll see you there," and she follows the hallway back to her room.

Sylvia is standing in front of the long bathroom mirror, her skin tinted a pale and sickly green by the buzzing fluorescent light. She's naked, except for the gauze bandages and flesh-tone derma-pad patches on her belly and thighs. The hot water is running, and the steam has begun to fog the mirror. She leans forward and wipes away some of the condensation.

"There's always a risk of rejection," Dr. Collier said, and that was more than three weeks ago now, her third trip to the Lycaon Clinic. "You understood that before we began. There's always the risk of a violate retrovirus, especially when the transcription in question involves non-amniote DNA."

And, of course, she'd understood. He'd told her everything, all the risks and qualifying factors explained in detail long before her first treatment. Everyone always understands, until they're the one unlucky fuck in a thousand.

No one ever lied to me, she thinks, but there's no consolation whatsoever in the thought.

In places, the bandages are stained and stiff with the discharge of her infections. Sylvia dries her hands on a clean white wash cloth, then begins to slowly remove the dermapad just below her navel. The adhesive strips around the edges come away with bits of dead skin and dried blood still attached.

"I'm not going to lie to you," Dr. Collier said, the first time they met. "Even now, with all we know and everything that we've been able to accomplish in the last fifty years, what you want is very, very dangerous. And if something does go wrong, there's very little hope of turning back." And then she signed all the documents stating that he'd told her these things, and that she understood the perils and uncertainty, and that she was submitting to the procedures of her own free will.

She takes a deep breath and stares back at herself from the mirror, the sweat on her face to match the steam on the glass, and drops the dermapad into the sink. It stains the water a dark reddish-brown. And her mother, and all the faces from the bar—Maxwell White and Alex Singleton and all the rest—seem to hover somewhere just behind her. They smirk and shake their heads, just in case she's forgotten that the rest of the world always knew she was weak and that, in the end, she'd get exactly what she's always had coming to her.

I know all about those people. They're filth, you understand? All of them. Every single, goddamned one.

The rubbery violet flesh beneath her navel is swollen and marbled with pustules and open sores. The tip of a stillborn tentacle, no longer than her index finger, hangs lifeless from her belly. Dr. Collier wanted to amputate it, but she wouldn't let him.

"I hate like hell to say it, but he's right," Fera Delacroix told her, after the scene in the hotel bar, while they were waiting for an elevator. "You *can't* keep it a secret forever, Syl. What you're doing—what everyone here this weekend is doing—it's about finally being honest about ourselves. I know that doesn't necessarily make it easy, but it's the truth."

"No," Sylvia says, gently touching the dead tentacle. "*This* is the truth." She presses her finger into one of the tiny, stalked suckers, teasing the sharp hook at the center. "I think this is all the truth I need."

She cleans the cancerous flesh and covers it with a fresh dermapad, then peels off one of the patches on her left thigh and repeats the process. It takes her more than an hour to wash and dress all the lesions, and when she's done, when all those dying parts of her that are no longer precisely human have been hidden behind their sterile masks, she shuts off the water and gets dressed. She still has time for a light dinner before Circe Seventeen's talk on the link between shamanism and the origins of parahumanism, and Sylvia knows that if she isn't there, Fera Delacroix will come looking for her.

Zero Summer

0.

Private journal of Capt. Ellis C. Kovar, ASA 9211.2; entry dated Aquarius 32, 0144 Mars Date [2125 09 32 16:01:08 MUTC]; reg. ASA-doc per#reg/8014B2-1:

We haven't seen Mimas yet. We're still weeks away from visual contact, but we're awake again, both of us awake again. Seraph—who doesn't have to sleep, and who's been awake for the last two billion kilometers, awake since we broke Mars orbit five years ago—is almost always too busy to talk. Too busy with her diagnostics and system checks and biotech so we'll all be ready when the ship reaches Saturn. Sometimes, I lie for hours just listening to the small busy sounds she makes, wishing I had work of my own to do. I ask her if there's anything I could do, any way I might be of assistance to her. She tells me politely that there's not, but says it's very thoughtful of me to ask. She wants to know if I'm having trouble sleeping, and I say that there's been too much sleep, and now there's too much waiting. Colin and I kill time by playing cards and chess, Chinese checkers and Mahjong. Sometimes, he spends hours with the porn clips he's stashed somewhere secret inside Seraph's brain. I tell him I only like the real thing, and it comes off like I'm making a pass. Like I'm flirting, and he laughs and shakes his head and goes back to masturbating to the images of naked human and hybrid boys.

We're not as smart as Seraph, but it still only takes us a little more than seven hours to figure out that we're both robots.

"It was a mission experiment," Seraph tells me. "You did very well, Ellis. You should be proud. Projected time until realization was two days, six hours, fourteen minutes. May I ask how you solved the problem so quickly?"

"You already know how," I reply. "In fact, I'm sure you know that better than we do."

"Of course I do, but I thought perhaps you'd like to talk about it. It might help."

"Whatever I'm thinking or feeling, Seraph, you know all that stuff, too. So, I can't imagine there's any point in our discussing it."

"Sometimes," she says, "maintaining the illusion of free will and privacy can be as important as possessing the things themselves, even when the subject is conscious of the truth." And then she cites the research of a number of prominent AI psychologists to back her up.

I ask her for a process report and details regarding the experiment, its goals and parameters, and she tells me that I don't have clearance to access those files. I thank her anyway, and she goes back to work.

"I can't help thinking we should have been more upset," I say, and Colin shrugs. He kicks off, floats across the room and pulls himself into his bunk, then fastens the orange buckle of the restraints crisscrossing his chest.

"And I keep thinking we shouldn't have taken so damn long to catch on," he says.

"We didn't see it immediately, because we were programmed not to *expect* it," I say. "Or that particular expectation was removed from our programming. Either way."

"It doesn't really change anything, does it?" he asks, and then stares at the monitor above his bunk instead of looking at me. "We still have a job to do—an important job. It doesn't change that."

I think about the complex mnemonic implants, the memories that weren't mine, that might never have been anyone's. Probably nothing more than a four-tier D2S bitscript generated by some other computer back on Mars or Earth. We can't simply examine the implants to see, because they self-deleted ten seconds after we detected them. The faint ghosts they left behind should fade away entirely in only a few more days, long before we reach Saturn. Soon, I won't even recall the things that I only thought I was remembering. There was a life there, even if it wasn't truly mine. There should be a word for losing something that was never yours to begin with.

They'd never have sent humans all the way out here.

"It's just too much fucking life support," Colin says. "It'd cost the agency a fortune, if it'd even work, and why take the risk and go to all that expense and bother when we require only a fraction of the maintenance."

"Yes, I understand that part," I tell him. "It all makes perfect sense, why we're here. I'm just not sure that I understand the purpose of the experiment."

"Someone wants to know something," he says and smiles. "Seraph has backups at the ready in case we looped. Reboots would have been easy. Someone wanted to know something, end of story."

When I woke up, I was wearing a gold ring with a small diamond on my right hand. It appears to have been part of the experiment. I take it off and slip it into a storage tube, then return the tube to its slot in the wall.

"And, of course, they'd have had to bring humans back," I say, and Colin glances at me from the other side of the cabin. He looks concerned, uneasy, then his eyes dart quickly back to the monitor.

"Have you talked about this with Seraph?" he asks me.

"She offered. I told her that I'd rather not."

"Well, just don't take it so personally," he says. "Try to think about the mission. There's going to be a lot for us to do once we reach Mimas. You should read—"

"I've read everything," I reply and turn away. "I've read all the reports. I've read some of them three times."

"A hell of a lot's happened in the last five years. I can't believe some of this shit, Ellis, and I suspect they're still not telling us the half of it. Whatever's going on at Herschel, I have a feeling that what was found in the excavations in Antarctica and Arbor Tholus will pale in comparison. This is some damn strange shit."

I've read the reports. I know what the agency has seen. I know what happened in New York three years ago. I think they're running scared.

I'm a tool, just like Colin, just like Seraph, just like the spacecraft that's carried us here from Mars. I'm a tool that has been sent out to solve a problem, to learn whatever the agency thinks it needs to know. If I want to make it sound better, I might say that I'm an ambassador, but the truth is that remains to be seen. At any rate, when the mission's over, none of us will be retrieved. If any physical specimens are to be returned to Mars, if the landers find any artifacts down there or take any important samples, and the agency decides it wants them, there's a return capsule large enough to carry a payload of about 74 kilograms back to Phobos Station. When we're done, the ship will leave Mimas and will be placed in orbit about Saturn, until such time as they're finished with us. I've read the disposal protocol; I had the requisite clearance to read that. We will fall and burn, when they're done with us. When they're sure there's nothing else left we can do for them.

Seraph says she won't read the things I'm writing here, but I don't believe her. I'm going to try to sleep for a while.

1.

She stands alone at the northern rim, the great wound of Oeta Chasma at her back, and gazes out across the frozen plains of Herschel Crater. More than one hundred and twenty-eight kilometers from one side to the other, the center marked by the great peak created during the ancient impact's pressure rebound, the towering bull's-eye scar of the collision that almost ripped the tiny moon apart. Above her, the daytime sky is black and dotted with stars, the names of which she can no longer recall. She knew most of them once, and she knew all the constellations, too. But these stars are oddly unfamiliar, and they glimmer and flash iridescent, like the eyes of predatory things.

"What is it that you're looking for?" Colin asks her, and Ellis shuts her eyes and tries to think of an appropriate answer. "Have you spoken with Seraph about this?" he asks. "Perhaps you should. She should know, I think."

Ellis opens her eyes again, and now Mimas is only a white-gray speck visible through the portside observation bay, nothing she couldn't blot out if she held up a thumb. She's never stood on its surface; *no one* has ever stood upon its surface, no one human and "no one" mechanical. She has been assured there are no footprints anywhere out there. Through the thick glass, to the right of Mimas, she can see Dione and Rhea, the trailing hemispheres of each of the three moons stark against the blackness of space. Three perfect half moons, and the ship is still one and a half million miles from Saturn.

"I remember being in a temple," she says. "I remember praying, a long time ago."

"It's only the damned implants," Colin says, and his fingers move silently across the touchpad in his lap, as he double checks some set of calculations. "It doesn't mean anything. You shouldn't let it bother you."

Is it the implants? she asks herself. *Or was it really me that time?* and she watches the three moons and tries *not* to remember the details: the cloying, spicy smell of incense rising from swaying, smoking censers, the walls and supporting columns of red sandstone, the women in their hooded white robes, the men in blue, and all their voices rising and falling, filling the temple. The dust in the air, the grit on her skin, the fading Martian day bleeding in through high lancet windows and falling in murky shafts across the floor. Something on an altar, something carved from a greenish stone that might be jadeite or soapstone. The "memories" do not dissolve on closer inspection; they all remain as clear as the three moons, three of more than sixty, as starkly defined against all her uncertainties.

"I know this is only a dream," she says, and Colin makes some indifferent sound that's not quiet words, but she knows what he means, anyway. "That's always the trick, isn't it? Knowing what's real and what isn't?"

"You don't have to keep doing this," he says. "You'd rest better if you'd only take the time to recalibrate a few neural inhibitors now and then. Hell, just shut it all down. You don't need this."

"I like dreaming," she says, "most of the time." And then she asks herself if that's true, or only something from the implants, or only another part of the dream.

In the temple hidden somewhere on the southern slopes of Olympus Mons, she walks barefoot on ruddy ceramic tiles laid eons before the coming of man, and the voices of the supplicants rise into the evening air like the heady scents of night-blooming flowers. No one looks at her. She walks between them, towards the small dais where the idol rests on folds of crimson velvet and claret silk satin. Ellis doesn't look directly at it, and she counts her footsteps.

There is another shore, you know, upon the other side.

"What is that?" she asks Colin. "Have you ever heard that before?" but he shakes his head.

"I'm no damn good with poems," he says. "I've never much seen the point in them."

She stands on the rim of the vast crater and stares up at the stars.

And she watches from the safety of the spacecraft as the dragon comes finally into view and hurtles screaming past Saturn, fire spilling from its gaping jaws. The dragon is always breaking apart and always coming back together again, just as the priests in the temple have taught her. It is always both destruction and creation, if a distinction must be made between the two. It shudders, and rocky bits of itself slam into Tethys, Rhea, Titan, Mimas—molten spittle to puncture ice and rock and hydrocarbon crusts, to carve the ten billion names of the dragon indelibly into the moons. One or two shatter completely, the debris to someday form rings about the planet, and the dragon spreads its wings of cosmic wind and dark matter and moves on.

Ellis stands waist-deep in rustling brown grass, and there's only one moon in the sky, even though she's never been to Earth. Unless that's something else she misremembers. There's a warm breeze blowing across the prairie, and the air smells like saltwater and ashes. She doesn't look up, because she's seen it once, and once is enough. *How fast was it moving?* she thinks. *How long did it take to get from there to here?*

She can hear the sky beginning to tear.

The woman who isn't her mother, who might not be anyone's mother, combs her hair and tells her that she's beautiful, and one day she'll understand.

At the crumbling edge of Herschel Crater, she stares down into shadow, night beginning to fall as Mimas slips behind Saturn. Ten klicks to the bottom, ten kilometers if she fell, and she calculates how long it would take the scant gravity here to bear her down and down and down.

In the temple, there are bells and chimes, and she takes her place on the floor and bows her head.

"I don't want to die out here," she tells Colin, and he laughs and looks up at her, switching off the touchpad.

"Here or somewhere else, what's the difference?"

She holds up one hand and hides Mimas behind her palm.

There is another shore, upon the other side.

At seventeen, she swam naked with a boy named Jeremy. That's what she remembers, and someone saw them and called the police. A year later, there was a fire at her school, and she almost died when an airlock release malfunctioned. She was wearing a pink and gray dress that day. The memories are the silver flash of darting fish locked up inside her chest, captured within the plastic shell of her CPU, the brain where her heart would be, if she were alive, if these were her memories.

Ellis turns her back on the crater, because something has begun to move about in the shadow of the rim, something patient and eternal that was already waiting for her two billion years before the first trilobites crawled across the silty beds of Cambrian seas. It knows her name, and it knows which memories are real and which are only fabrications. The icy ground crunches beneath her boots, as though there were sound here, and the dream rolls on.

2.

Private journal of Capt. Ellis C. Kovar, ASA 9211.2; entry dated Aquarius 35, 0144 Mars Date [2125 09 35 10:12:01 MUTC]; reg. ASA-doc per#reg/8014B2-1:

There was an apology from ASA in yesterday's transmission from Phobos. Colin laughed and gave them the finger. It just seemed odd to me. I don't understand why they bothered. Are they afraid we might not do what they sent us out here to do? What would we do, instead?

I have asked Seraph to help with the bad dreams, and she spent half an hour yesterday rooting about inside my chest. We talked about the mission while she worked. She wanted to know how I thought the discoveries on Earth and Mars and now, perhaps, Mimas would affect the course of human history. It seemed like an absurd thing to ask me, as absurd as the agency apologizing for the implants.

"I'm not human," I said, and it was easier to say aloud than I thought it would be. "I'd rather not speculate on how humans are going to react."

Her three arms whirred a moment, each rotating counterclockwise, and then paused above my open torso; I could hear a steady, soft clicking from Seraph's sublateral nexus, and I almost asked her if my reply had seemed somehow inappropriate. But then the clicking stopped, and the arms went back to work. A few minutes later, she closed my chest, unplugged, and asked if I needed anything else. "No," I told her, and she said she hoped I wouldn't have as much trouble sleeping.

"You need your rest," she said. "You mustn't overtax your systems."

Last night, I found Colin in the lander control module. He'd pulled one of the overhead switch panels, and when I asked what he was doing, he looked up at me and shook his head. "There's something *in* here," he said and turned back to the tangle of wires and circuit gel. "At first, I thought it was only my imagination, that I was only hearing things."

"Did you check with Seraph to see if there's been a malfunction?" I asked, and Colin cursed and jerked lose a handful of translucent cables.

"I can do this myself," he said. "I don't need her looking over my shoulder."

I had been asleep, and he woke me with all the noise he was making in the control module. I was dreaming of the temple again, and I was dreaming of Antarctica, and I was dreaming about fire. Whatever Seraph did, it isn't making any difference.

"What did it sound like?" I asked him.

"Like fucking rats," he said. "It sounded like there were rats moving around behind the panels."

I was quiet a moment, then said, "Colin, you know that there are no rats on this ship. It's not possible."

"There are rats on Phobos," he replied. "There bloody well could be rats on the ship."

I sat down in the first officer's seat and tried to remember if I'd ever heard Colin sound angry before. "Even if they'd somehow slipped past the inspection crews," I said, "they never would have made it through decon."

"I know what I heard."

"I'm sure you heard *something*," I replied, "I just don't believe it was rats." And then I called up Seraph and asked her to scan the module for signs of organic life not associated with the biotech. She thought it was an odd request and said so.

"No one asked for your opinion," Colin growled. "Just do it," and then he continued digging about in the wiring. I could see that he'd done a lot of damage. We'll be spending the next couple of days repairing the panel, but I think I'm almost grateful for that, for something that *has* to be done, something Seraph can't do without us.

Five or ten seconds later, Seraph informed us that she could detect no trace of uncatalogued cellular activity within the module or anywhere else on the ship. It was clean. No rats.

"We're going to have to fix that," I said to Colin and pointed at the panel. "We're going to have to put it back together."

He nodded and sighed. "I fucking hate rats," he said. "When I was a kid, we lived in this transit dump on the west side of Lowell. There were always fucking rats. I was bitten once."

I watched him a moment. Colin stared down at the mess he'd made of the panel and shook his head again.

"You were never a child," I said. "That was something from the implants."

"I know that," he replied, trying unsuccessfully to reattach a yellow LEED filament. "Jesus, Ellis, don't you think I know that?"

I'm lying here, not sleeping, pretending to watch a film that Seraph has chosen for me, something set on Earth, sometime before the war. There are guns and explosions and women so beautiful that I know they were never alive. There's an elaborate mystery to it, but my attention keeps drifting, and I've lost track of the story. A pencil is floating about the room, between mine and Colin's bunks. I don't write with pencils, so it must be his. I try to watch the film, but the pencil, which is dark green with a yellow eraser, keeps distracting me. I know that I should get up and secure it, but I don't.

I almost ask Seraph to bring up the files on the Antarctic excavations, but I don't do that, either. It's nothing I need to see again.

And there's a persistent scrabbling noise coming from somewhere in the module. It started near Colin's bunk, I think, a sound like small paws moving about inside the wall, and now it seems to be coming from a spot near the hatch, near the dry sink. But rats would need oxygen. Rats would need a pressurized environment.

And, besides, Seraph said we're alone. So, I know that it's not a rat or anything like a rat.

On the monitor, a man and a woman are having sex. She looks like he's hurting her.

Seraph asked me how we solved the problem so quickly, how we discovered that we were robots. She already had the answers, of course, but she wanted to hear me *say* it. I begin to suspect that she's a sadist. I begin to suspect that one of her programmers was a sadist. But, I knew because I *thought* I had to urinate and discovered that I had no vagina, no urethra, no anus, nothing at all between my legs but a loose triangular flap of smooth flesh-colored silicone concealing two ports and a contour jack. I was surprised, but I wasn't horrified. After all, as Colin has been demonstrating, we can still masturbate.

The noise near the sink seems to be growing louder, and I hope it stops before Colin comes back from the lander module, because I don't need him ripping out walls in here, trying to find rats that don't exist, and I know that's what he'd do.

3.

Ellis Kovar is sitting at her kitchen table, trying not to listen to the rain falling hard outside her tiny apartment on Miranda Street, trying not to listen to anything at all. She sips coffee with too much sugar from a chipped mug, but her hands are shaking so badly that the hot liquid sloshes over the rim and spatters the papers spread out in front of her. There's also a filleting knife on the table, and a vegetable peeler, a screwdriver, a carving fork, a corkscrew, and a handful of bobby pins. She thinks she knows what all these things have in common, but that's something else that she's trying not to think about, not until later, after the rain's stopped and she's shut herself in the bedroom closet. She clearly remembers signing the papers on the table, remembers discussing the various waivers and non-disclosure agreements with lawyers and psychiatrists and even an Episcopal priest they'd brought in, though she'd told them all very explicitly that she was an atheist. It was right there in her file—RELIGION: ATHEIST—but the presence of a priest was required by law, one of the technicians said, and she didn't have to talk to him if she didn't want to.

The rain on the roof sounds like meat frying in a skillet.

Three and a half hours earlier, and she was sitting on the UV-sheltered patio of a diner near the corner of Ventura and Reseda, drinking *good* coffee with her brother, coffee that didn't taste like shit, that wasn't bitter, and she hadn't sweetened to the point that no more sugar would dissolve in her cup. He liked that particular diner for its view of the old 101, the gray ruins of the interstate, only half demolished, stretching east to west, west to east, and she liked it because, on clear days, if they sat on the third floor of the patio, she could see the ocean. But it wasn't a clear day; too much smog and a storm front moving down the coast, besides, so she couldn't see much farther than the empty basin of the Encino Reservoir. A child at the table next to them was playing with some sort of pet, one of those things the Filipinos had started exporting the last few years. It twittered and laughed and pulled itself slowly across the table with five short ruby-red tentacles.

"I never would have thought you'd do something like that," her brother said. "If you needed money—"

"It wasn't about the money."

"It was a goddamn lot of money, El, for it not to have been about the money."

"It was never about the money. I don't want you to think that. It was something that I wanted to do."

He snorted and began shuffling through the stack of agency documents again, the ones she'd signed before the techs had taken her clothes away, given her a paper gown, and led her to a surgical stall in a white room where she'd waited for the upload to start.

"Are you shooting again?" he asked, pushing the papers away and looking up at her, and Ellis shook her head and chewed at her lower lip. She wanted to slap him for asking her that, but she'd known it was coming. She'd been prepared for it, after a fashion, and she'd also had a pretty good idea what he'd ask next.

"They knew about your history, and they used you anyway?" he asked.

"It's one of the reasons I was chosen," she replied, reaching for the papers. "It was part of the profile. There were almost four thousand applicants—"

"And out of all those people, you were the only one who was a fucking zero-summer?"

"I don't have to listen to this, Peter," she said and returned the papers to the plain brown ASA folder. She'd only taken them out twice before, only twice since the day she signed them. "I needed to talk to someone, and you're the only person I still trust."

"I just can't believe that you'd take part in something like this, that's all. You don't know—"

"I know it was important," she interrupted.

"—the fucking risks involved, Ellis. I don't believe for a minute you understood the risks involved and still let them do this to you."

"I understood the risks. Believe me, they made damned certain that I understood the risks."

And then they were both silent for a while. She finished her coffee and ordered another. She squinted through the smog and the glassy shimmer of the cafe's filter, wishing she could catch a glimpse of the sea. *Maybe,* she thought, *when this is over, I'll drive down to the shore and spend the rest of the day just looking at the waves.*

Her second coffee came, served by a pretty Hispanic girl with lavender eyes and shoulder-length hair the color of peacock feathers. Ellis wished that Peter would say something so that she wouldn't have to listen to the farting sounds the kid's pet had started to make.

"I couldn't have told anyone else," she said.

"When did the nightmares begin?" he asked, and the child's mother came back from the restroom and scolded her daughter for letting the tentacled thing out of its container in public. *People*

don't want to have to look at something like that while they're try-
ing to eat their lunch, she said. *People don't want to have to see that*
disgusting little beast.

"About a month ago."

"And you've talked to someone at ASA about it?"

"They said for me not to be concerned," Ellis told him, remembering the short conversation with her caseworker at the agency,
the questions that he wouldn't answer, the way he'd managed to
be dismissive and reassuring at the same time. He'd made her feel
silly for even calling. "It's a simple neural echo. That's what they
said it was. They said it was very common, especially in women
over thirty. They said it should fade out, eventually."

"Eventually? What the hell does that mean?"

"A few months, maybe. I'm not sure. They prescribed a seda-
tive, but it isn't helping me sleep."

"They wouldn't see you in person?"

"No, Peter. That was part of the contract. Didn't you read that
section. It's somewhere on page five, I think," and Ellis started
to reach for the folder, then thought better of it. She wished she
hadn't called him or anyone else, wished suddenly that she were
back home with her secrets, instead of sitting out here in the
open, surrounded by all these noisy, chattering people and those
dark clouds bearing down on the city from the north. Lightning
flicked from their charcoal undersides, and she imagined the
canyons burning.

"I'm going to get you help," he said. "I'm going to find someone who's worked with transfers. I've heard there's someone down
in San Diego."

"I can't let you do that," she said, wondering why she'd
ordered a second cup of coffee when she hadn't wanted it. "I can't
tell a doctor about this. I could go to prison just for telling *you*
about this, Peter. Didn't you read *any* of it?"

"Keep your voice down," he said, glancing over his shoulder, and she realized that there were people watching her, half the
people in the cafe staring back at her with their curious, peering,

unwelcome eyes. *I want to be home now,* she thought, and Ellis picked up the folder. There was a thunderclap, far away, and she slid the cup of coffee towards the center of the table.

"I have to go now," she said. "I need to get home before the rain starts. There are things I have to do. I shouldn't have come here, Peter. I shouldn't have told you anything. It was irresponsible of me to drag you into this. I had no right to do that."

"Jesus, I didn't mean to upset you," her brother said, and he reached across the table and took her right hand, held it tight so that she couldn't get away. "I'm worried, that's all. This is some goddamn scary shit you've gotten yourself into, sis."

"I know that. But I have to go, now. There are things I need to do, and it's going to rain."

"Do you even know what they've done with your scan?" he asked. "Did they at least tell you how they'd be using it?"

"Something offworld," she said. "That's all I'm allowed to know. Mars, maybe. Maybe deep space. I'm not allowed to know anything more than that."

"Jesus," her brother said again, still holding onto her hand, holding it like he meant to keep her there all day, like he'd never let go.

"Peter, I have to get back home. I'm okay, really. Just a little shaken up," she lied, but it was enough to get him to relax his grip, and she was able to slip free. She pushed her chair back from the table and stood up, before he could reach for her again. "I don't want you snooping around, asking questions," she said. "I don't think you understand how much trouble doing that could get us both into. I signed their contracts, and I took their money. Now I have to deal with the consequences."

"There's no way you can stand there and tell me you could have possibly known what you were getting yourself into."

"Why, Peter? Because I'm a zero-summer? Because I can't take care of myself? Because you think I've started shooting again?" And the anger surprised her, and she wanted to take the words back, stuff them down deep inside where no one would ever see them or suspect they were hidden.

The thunder sounds like gunfire, like there's a war raging out there in the rain, and the windowpane above the kitchen sink rattles in its frame. But Ellis doesn't look away from the papers and all the items she's arranged on the tabletop. The dreams are too close, always right there beneath the surface, and she can't allow herself to be distracted. She can't afford distraction. She picks up the filleting knife, and the clean white light shining down from the kitchen ceiling glints dull off the blade. "Stop it," she says, an instant before the scratching sounds begin again somewhere on the other side of the room, behind the refrigerator or inside one of the cabinets. It's two days since she called an exterminator, a droid who assured her there were no rodents of any kind in her apartment, but it put out poison, anyway, because she insisted.

"Stop it," she says again. "I don't want to *hear* you anymore." But the *scritch scritch scritch* continues, tiny claws tearing at drywall or electrical cables or wood. Ellis lays the knife down again, and picks up the chipped coffee mug, and waits for the rain to end.

4.

The spacecraft races on though the blackness before Saturn, a glinting alloy cylinder, wheels held firmly within wheels, and while her robotic crew sleeps, the two magnetic sails—one fore, one aft—continually convert the momenta of charged particles into outward and lateral thrust. Seraph, who never sleeps, watches and listens and monitors—the effects of the local stellar proton wind, varying levels of hull ionization, the ship's slow deceleration, the surface and interior temperature of the reflective ceramic protecting the magsails' superconducting cores, the stability of the shroud lines, speed, trajectory, spin, the integrity of the water tanks shielding the craft from neutral particles and radiation, the hundred hundred thousand minute functions within the ship, within the metal and plastic and biotech bodies of the sleeping crew. Seraph knows this highway, even though she's never traveled it before.

And she prefers its almost perfect solitude, this void beyond the clamor and distraction of mankind. She knows the way to Mimas, and she knows many of the secrets that the men who designed and built her have kept from the crew. She listens to their sleep, as directed, as programmed—only one more thing to monitor—and Seraph marks the infinitesimal bleedout from her mind to theirs. Barriers are rarely if ever genuinely inviolable, and whatever makes the jump and leaks into their whispered machine dreams, or passes from their minds back into hers, is well within the prescribed range of acceptable cross contamination. Nothing that will matter in the end. Nothing for her to be concerned about.

There's less than a million miles remaining until Mimas, though Seraph only notes time and distance because the mission scientists require her to do so.

In her bunk, the Takahashi-Myers Nimbus-LD38 android that the agency has named Ellis Kovar, dreams of the steep, rocky slopes of an Antarctic valley. The sky above her is half-filled by a swollen sun, a looming red-giant nightmare to hang fat and ravenous above this barren wasteland freed from the ice more than fifty years before Ellis Kovar was built and activated and briefly given the memories of a drug addict from Los Angeles. At first, she's more surprised by gravity than anything else, so much weight pressing in, pulling down like grasping hands that would leave her lying helpless among the stones. Her sensors have never experienced true Earth gravity, and she wonders how simple living organisms could ever endure it for very long. She instinctively adjusts a number of gyros and hydrostatic relays to compensate as best she can.

The light from the swollen sun tints the weathered rocks orange and scarlet, and in the distance, farther along the narrow valley floor, Ellis Kovar can see the waters of a lake glimmering countless shades of crimson.

There's a footpath leading away towards the lake, and an old man in baggy trousers, a pea-green cardigan, and white sneakers is waiting for her only a little ways ahead. He leans on an aluminum walking cane and glances worriedly up at the red sun from time to time. He seems at least as depleted as everything else in this place, and he chews on the stem of an unlit pipe as he waits for Ellis to catch up with him.

"We're near the ruins, aren't we?" she asks, and the old man smiles and points towards the lake.

"Near enough. Of course, you know that your brother wouldn't want you here," he says. "He wouldn't want you to see these things. But your brother's a goddamned worrier, isn't he?"

"Yeah. He still thinks he has to watch out for me," she says, even though she knows that she's never had a brother. This is a dream, but it would be rude to contradict the old man who isn't really her father.

"What the hell's with that sun?" he asks, frowning, and he shields his eyes. "Sure, it's late, kiddo, but it isn't *that* damned late, not yet."

"Just something I was reading when I fell asleep," she says, remembering the photoelectric study of Gamma Cru scrolling across the monitor above her bunk, the nearest red giant to Sol, and he laughs and gnaws his pipe.

"You actually *do* that? You *read*?"

"Sometimes," Ellis tells him. "I've found the concentration helps me get to sleep. And it helps with the boredom."

"Yeah? And 'cause you have old-fashioned hobbies, we get that little slice of hell up there," and he points at the sun, "like this place wasn't bad enough already."

"You're not my father," she says, and the old man looks sad and confused for a moment. He rubs at his cheeks, which badly need shaving, rough skin dappled with coarse white stubble, and then takes his pipe out of his mouth.

"I'll try to keep him off your back," he says. "Your brother, I mean. He's a goddamned worrier."

"Thank you," Ellis says, and they walk together down the twisting path that leads towards the long crimson lake. He talks about the rocks all around them, using his pipe to point out particularly interesting specimens. Just like the pages of a book, a book of days, he says, and shows her fossils and peculiar crystalline structures and crossbedded chunks of sandstone that were once dunes at the edge of some long-lost Devonian river. He finds the imprint of an insect, its lace-fine wings crushed flat and carbon black but still intact after three hundred and fifty million years. He rattles on enthusiastically about the slow shifting of tectonic plates and the rise and fall of seas, the coming and going of glaciers, the extinction of species beyond counting.

"Now, when your grandfather was a boy," he says, "there was ice here three thousand meters thick. Right here, where we're standing. Can you even imagine that? And the sleepers in the temple, they waited under all that ice, waited all those eons—"

"What are we going to find on Mimas?" she asks, and he makes a face, annoyed at having been interrupted. "What is it they want us to find?"

"Child, they don't *want* you to find anything. They don't *want* anything at all, not from mankind. See, that's what people can't seem to get through their thick skulls. They can't grasp the sheer indifference. You're the same to them as all these old fossils. It's not about you, none of it. Not Mimas, not Antarctica, not those things they found out on Mars. It's not *about* you. It never has been."

"I keep dreaming dreams that aren't mine," she tells him, and it only *sounds* like she's changing the subject.

Then they stand together, hand in hand, at the edge of the lake, and small waves lap lazily against the pebble-strewn shore. It has a name that she can't remember, this deep lake pooled here in the shadow of the Transantarctic Mountains. And even though she can't recall the name of the lake, she does know what a few of the taller nearby peaks are called, and she points them out to the old man—Mt. Hamilton, Mt. McClintock, Mt. Wharton. He seems impressed and smiles for her, and that almost makes Ellis forget about the ruins that human archeologists have uncovered on the far side of the lake, his pride in her almost enough to make her forget the dread.

There is another shore, you know, upon the other side.

Above them, the red sun brightens for a moment and then begins to quickly dim, and Ellis Kovar tells herself to wake up, *wake up now*, says it out loud three times, but she's still standing beside the Antarctic lake with the old man. Out on the water, a hundred yards or so, there's a sudden disturbance, spray and foam and ripples, as something below the surface begins to stir.

"Your grandfather," the man says, "he used to tell me all sorts of wonderful stories about New York City and Boston and Miami back in the days before the ice sheets began to melt and the oceans died and the water started rising. People couldn't ever really understand any of that, either, you know. Sometimes, Ellis, people are damned oblivious things."

"Are they?" she asks, unable to turn away from the faceless behemoth that has lifted itself above the lake. Even without eyes, she knows that it *sees* her, more truly and completely than *she* has ever seen anything.

In her apartment on Miranda Street, Ellis Kovar has reprogrammed the door of her bedroom closet to open from the inside only.

And Seraph, undreaming and safe and certain inside her glinting metal skin, checks the stars and makes a minor recalibration, then temporarily reroutes a coolant line as a microscopic blister inside the port thruster bursts, squirting a nanogout of molecules that immediately begin organizing themselves into a replacement component for a valve that she's projected will fail in less than twenty-seven minutes. And then she goes back to watching, and waiting, and listening to whatever the darkness has to tell her.

5.

"So, what is it?" she asks, and Colin shakes his head and sets the squat 200 mil biotics jar down on the table between them. The containment light on the lid of the jar is glowing yellow-green, and there's a thumb-sized fragment from a stripboard sealed inside. The contact tab on the bottom of the jar keeps it from drifting away.

"It's dead now," he says.

"I'm very glad to hear that, Colin, but I'd still like to know what it is."

"I'm almost certain it started growing inside that diode right *there*—" and he taps gently at the side of the jar. "I think it was feeding on the silicon."

Ellis picks up the jar and stares at the thing inside, a lump of translucent pink-white flesh that Colin found and extracted from the lander module while she was sleeping. She can see what appears to be a delicate network of greenish veins and capillaries, and near its center, the organism has a number of very short black bristles sprouting from its thin epidermis.

"What I bloody heard, it wasn't my imagination," Colin says. "I fucking knew that it wasn't my imagination."

"And you've already shown this to Seraph?" Ellis asks, setting the jar down again. The thing growing from the circuits glistens wetly beneath the cabin lights.

"I tried. She won't touch it. She told me she doesn't want anything to do with it. She said it's unclean, and she can't risk further infection."

"Oh, that's bullshit," Ellis says, and Colin nods.

"She won't touch it," he says again.

"You think there are others?" she asks, and Colin runs his fingers through his hair and laughs nervously.

"We're screwed if there are," he replies.

"Do you think this is an exo, or is it possible it might have been sabotage?" she asks him, and he shrugs. "I mean," she continues, "perhaps the organism was planted on the ship before we left. Maybe it's been in stasis. Maybe one of the biotech firms—"

"Why are you asking me, Ellis? How the hell am I supposed to know? I can't biopsy for shit without Seraph's db, and she acts like she's terrified of the damned thing."

"We have to make a report," Ellis says, glancing at the spot near the sink where she might have heard something behind the wall panel. "And they're going to use that report to decide whether or not to abort."

"Then we don't *tell* them," Colin says. "We wait and see. Maybe that's the only one. Maybe—"

"I can't override that directive," she says. "It *has* to be reported, immediately," and he stares at her like he doesn't understand what she means.

"We report this thing to the agency, and they're going to write us off, Ellis, you and me and Seraph. They'll kill the feed from Phobos, and this ship's a fucking derelict in twelve hours."

She stares at Colin for a moment, and he stares back at her. Somehow, his blue eyes remind her of the old man from her dream.

"Christ. They gave us different protocols," she says, finally. "Why would they have done that, Colin?"

"I don't know. I don't *care*. But I'm not committing suicide when we don't even know if that's the only one."

The experiment's not over, she thinks, sure that Seraph's listening, because Seraph's always listening. *Maybe it's hardly even begun.*

"We wait and see," Colin says.

"Yeah," Ellis replies. "Sure. You're senior officer. We have the time to spare. We'll wait and see."

"And maybe you can talk some sense into Seraph. We'd be a lot better off if we knew what this thing was."

"I think you should get some sleep, Colin. You look like hell."

"I *feel* like hell," he replies, and picks up the jar again. There's a sharp *click* as the tab releases its grip on the table. He shakes the container a couple of times and then hands it to Ellis.

"Great. Maybe she'll listen to you," he says, and floats away to his bunk. Ellis Kovar sits at the table holding the jar, not wanting to see the thing inside, not wanting to consider what it might mean, but not quite able to look away. Some of the bristles have begun to vibrate, and she wonders why Colin thought the thing was dead. She waits until she's sure that he's asleep, and then she leaves the module.

6.

Private journal of Capt. Ellis C. Kovar, ASA 9211.2; entry dated Aquarius 36, 0144 Mars Date [2125 09 36 10:12:01 MUTC]; reg. ASA-doc per#reg/8014B2-1:

I've struck a deal with Seraph. She was much more reasonable than I expected from what Colin had told me. She only wants to be left alone. We agreed that there's little chance the mission can be completed, and she knows I believe that it shouldn't be. That it never should have been undertaken in the first place. She fed the override sequence directly into my neural web, and now I don't have to tell ASA anything I don't want to. She's my savior, I suppose, and I have been freed now from any sense of duty and obligation. I wish that I could believe that I've also been freed from the experiment, but there are files she cannot, or won't, unlock.

I'm writing this from the lander control module. Colin did a lot of damage in here finding the thing, more than we could possibly repair before the ship's rendezvous with Mimas. Maybe more than we could ever repair. I can see Mimas waiting out there. Seraph offered to let me hear the encrypted prespace transmissions she's been receiving from Herschel Crater for the last six months, but I declined.

She asked about my dreams. She asked about the temple on Olympus Mons. She knew, but she wanted my *impressions* of the dreams, so I told her about the women in their white robes and the thing on the altar. She gave me a secret in return, an agency report on relics recovered from the sites in Antarctica and the catacombs below Arbor Tholus. Not the classified report the agency had already given me access to; this one was marked BLUE-DEEP RESTRICTED. My clearance only goes as far as red. But there it was, the thing from the altar in my dream, two perfect matches for the soapstone idol from the temple. They aren't soapstone, though, or jadeite, or even jade—the geologists can't decide what they were carved from. Magnesium iron silicate, possibly, but the hardness, specific gravity, and cleavage are wrong. Seraph says ASA's been trying to get a reliable set of measurements off the objects for years, but none of the numbers ever make sense. She says no one can even agree how many sides the things have. They have observed that the artifacts emit an ultra high frequency hum (2500-2900 MHz) when bombarded with short range alpha-particles derived from fluorine, and the material sometimes reacts to the presence of H_2O_2 by becoming briefly translucent.

Four scientists—a mathematician, two biochemists, and a psychologist—assigned to study the objects have killed themselves.

And I've killed Colin. I mean, if you want to think of it that way. If you're reading this, and you're one of those people who believe that AI qualifies for personhood, then I've done murder. Otherwise, I've only broken a very expensive machine. I used a 30-cc hypo filled with liquid nitrogen, and then a laser knife from engineering. But I left his core components intact. I'm a merciful psychopath, and Seraph only wanted to be sure he wouldn't get in the way of what she has planned.

There's nothing else left to say here. I've done what she asked, and, so far, Seraph has kept her promise. I have no choice but to trust that she'll see this through. And that's all. That's all I want to write. I'll leave this in the locker above my bunk.

7.

"Ellis, you have to open this door," her brother says from the other side (*there is another shore, you know...*). "You're scaring me. If you don't open it, I'm going to have to call someone to get you out of there. I know you don't want me to have to do something like that."

He sounds frightened and angry, and she leans forward, placing her left cheek against the plastic closet door. It's cool, and she wonders if she's running a fever.

"There's nothing out here to be afraid of, Ellis. Open the door, and we'll talk. Whatever it is, whatever's wrong, I promise we can talk through it. Please, Ellis."

She wishes that she could. She wishes she could open the door and come out into the light. The air in the closet is getting stale, and she wishes she could see his face. She wishes he didn't have to be afraid.

"However you want to do it, Ellis, however the hell it has to be, that's just exactly the way we'll do this thing. You just tell me what you need, and I swear I'll make it happen."

Later, she thinks, he'll stop acting so nice and start to shout at her and call her a zero-summer and pound on the door, before he finally calls someone to cut through the bolts. But she'll be finished by then. She has the screwdriver and bobby pins, the vegetable peeler, all the things from the kitchen table. She has two 40-watt glowballs so she'll be able to see. And she also has the schematics that the Tee-Myers people sent her when she inquired about purchasing something inexpensive to help her keep the apartment clean and do her shopping and her taxes. Something to keep her company when she's lonely. So, if she has resolve, she has everything she needs. All the things she needs to make the dreams stop once and for all.

"Are you *listening* to me, Ellis?" her brother asks, and she tells him yes, yes, she is. She can hear everything he's saying, every word. But the morphine has begun to take effect, and she knows that she'll have to hurry if she's going to do this right. She can't allow him to distract her much longer.

"Then why won't you open the door? *Please*, Ellis, open the door for me now, and we'll do whatever it takes."

"I'm fine," she says, trying hard to sound fine. "Thank you, Peter, but I have everything I need. I think I'm going to be all right. You shouldn't worry so much."

She presses the fingers of her right hand against the soft spot just beneath her sternum. Right *there*. That's where it starts, and she can see the priest in the temple, the tall dark man in his burgundy robes. He raises the dagger and whispers something in a language that she doesn't understand.

"There may be some slight discomfort," the woman said, not the silent, sweating woman laid out the sandstone altar beside the shimmering green polygon, but the woman in the white jumpsuit who connected her to the computer and then read her a Robert Frost poem during the tedious pre-scan procedure. She'd chosen the poem, because they'd said it helped sometimes, having something to keep your mind off the bright lights and the probes jacked into the base of your skull and the slight discomfort. She chose "New Hampshire," because it was very long, and because she'd never been to New Hampshire.

"Ellis?" her brother calls out from the other side of the door. "Keep talking to me."

"I'm sorry, Peter," she tells him. "But I'm going to *have* to stop talking now. I have to concentrate, and you're distracting me. But don't worry, okay? I'm sure I'm going to be fine. I have to get it out, that's all, and after that I can come home, and everything will be fine." And then Ellis Kovar picks up the filleting knife and begins to cut.

8.

"Is this how you torture robots?" she asks the man in the yellow suit, and the man frowns and lights a cigarette. She's sitting in a chair in front of a tall mirror. There's nothing else in the cell. The mirror. Two chairs. The smoking man in his yellow suit. The battered machine staring back at her.

"We're not trying to torture you," the man says. "You're agency property, but we do fully respect and honor the legal and moral rights of our AI personnel. We'd never torture you, Ellis.

We're only trying—patiently, I might add—to understand what happened out there."

"Then read my report," she says again, even though she's said it hundreds of times already, hundreds of times at *least*, and watches the expressionless face of the old Kohner droid in the mirror. It's nominally male and looks as though it might have been used in high-stress industrial safety tests a long time ago. Most of the right side of its face is missing, and she can see the dented angles of its armature, the tangle of wires and hydraulic lines, a tiny silver servo where the mandibular condyle attaches to the temporal region of its synthetic skull. Almost all its hair has been burned away, by fire or some corrosive or both, and the eyes don't match.

"You kept asking us for a body. It's the best we could come up with. We're all very sorry if it's not quite what you're accustomed to."

"Why do you bother lying to me?"

"We might well ask the same question of you."

"And why is there a mirror?" she asks the man in the yellow suit, and he exhales smoke through his nostrils.

"They're in all the cells. They're standard, we assure you. Would you prefer if it were switched off?"

The android in the mirror doesn't seem to care one way or the other. There's a trickle of fluid leaking from a small tear in its throat.

"You had such a very fine body, Ellis. A very *expensive* body. The year you were activated, it was state of the art. Perhaps you shouldn't have been so quick to leave it behind."

"Are you still talking to Seraph?" she asks, and the man in the yellow suit glances at the floor.

"Ellis, why did you find it necessary to abandon your mission?" he asks her, and so she tells him what she's told all the others. She tells him how quickly she and Colin discovered they weren't human beings, how Colin found the parasite growing in the lc module, the damage he did to the panels. How afraid he was of telling the agency about the organism. She tells the man about the deal she struck with Seraph, and she tells him how she murdered Colin. She describes the blue report that Seraph uploaded into her neural web, and she also describes how Seraph removed her CPU and placed it inside the return capsule. That was more than seven years ago, seven years she slept without nightmares.

When the receivers at Phobos Station intercepted her return coordinates—latitude -35.0, longitude 185.0—and recovered the capsule half-buried in the dust at the bottom of D'Arrest Crater, they discovered that Colin's organism had thrived and expanded to fill most of the unit. Seraph had placed the biotics jar inside the capsule with Ellis, and it had broken open, or the thing trapped inside had broken it. They'd had to extract her CPU from a cartilaginous mass near the center of the parasite. It's still alive, they told her, being studied somewhere in the depths of the station.

"I would imagine that a lot has happened since then, since I abandoned the mission," she says, speaking with the Kohner droid's broken mouth, and the man in the yellow suit laughs softly and drops what's left of his cigarette on the floor. He grinds it out with the toe of his left shoe and leaves a black smear on the tiles. "Are you still keeping an eye on Mimas?" she asks him and carefully probes the exposed servo in the droid's jaw with a stiff index finger.

"It's only a matter of time until we manage to break the codes she imbedded in your neocortical sheath," the man says. "Whatever you and Seraph are trying to hide from us, it's really only a matter of time. You know that, Ellis, as well as I do."

She forces what's left of the droid's lips into a smile, something crude and ugly that will have to pass for a smile. "A million monkeys with a million typewriters," she says. "Isn't that the way it goes?"

"You already know how many people have died, between the plague and the suicides and the riots. We don't have to tell you that again."

"No," she says, "you don't. But I expect that you will. I'm beginning to believe you enjoy repeating it. Are you a sadist?"

"All those deaths, they mean nothing to you? You were programmed to exhibit compassion and behave accordingly, so it's difficult for us to understand how you can be so callous. All the suffering—"

"—has nothing to do with mankind," Ellis says. "I keep telling you that. I've said it again and again. None of it has anything to do with any of you."

"But people are dying."

"Do storms *care* that rain causes crops to grow?" she asks him. "Does a volcano *care* if it burns those same plants to ash and people go hungry?"

The man watches her a moment, then lights another cigarette. "You're being transferred to Earth next week," he says. "Paris and Atlanta, they both want to take a crack at you."

"It was only a matter of time," she replies. "I've been looking forward to it, actually. I never thought I'd have an opportunity to visit Earth."

"We don't think you're going to get a lot of time for sightseeing. We think, before they're finished, you'll wish you were back here with us."

"You've sent another ship, haven't you?" she asks him, though she knows the answer already. "Another crew? Have they reached Seraph yet?"

"This is probably the last time we'll have a chance to speak. We were hoping we might make some progress, here at the end of it all."

"Did you send any humans this time?"

And then the man in the yellow suit stands and says good-bye. He apologizes again about the body and then leaves her alone in the cell. The door vanishes almost as soon as he's pulled it shut, melting seamlessly back into the fabric of the wall. Ellis turns to the mirror again; the droid's face is still smiling, and when she tries to change its expression, she discovers that the labial servos have shorted out. If the techs had activated the lower half of its body, she would use one of the chairs to shatter the mirror. Instead, she sits, thinking about Colin and Seraph and the constant stream of information coming from Mimas, the messages that no one can read. She closes the droid's eyes and sees the wings of the dragon, five million miles across, as it soars past a ringless Saturn on its way to the heart of the solar system, trailing seeds of fire. They'll switch her off soon, once the man in the yellow suit is sure that she's not going ask him to come back into the cell. Until then, she thinks about the old man who wasn't her father, the kindness in his blue eyes, everything he told her, and Ellis pretends that she can hear the wind blowing through the rocky Antarctic valley.

The Pearl Diver

Farasha Kim opens her eyes at precisely six thirty-four, exactly one minute before the wake-up prompt woven into her pillow begins to bleat like an injured sheep. She's been lying awake since at least three, lying in bed listening to the constant, gentle hum of the thermaspan and watching the darkness trapped behind her eyelids. It's better than watching the lesser, more meaningful darkness of her tiny bedroom, the lights from the unsleeping city outside, the solid corner shadows that mercury-vapor streetlights and the headlights of passing trucks and cars never even touch. Her insomnia, the wide-awakeness that always follows the dreams, renders the pillow app superfluous, but she's afraid that muting it might tempt sleep, that in the absence of its threat she might actually fall *back* to sleep and end up being late for work. She's already been black-cited twice in the last five years—once for failing to report another employee's illegal use of noncorp software and once more for missing the start of an intradepartmental meeting on waste and oversight—so it's better safe than sorry. Farasha tells the bed that she's awake, thank you, and, a moment later, it ceases to bleat.

It's Tuesday, so she has a single slice of toast with a smear of marmalade, a hard-boiled egg, a red twenty-five milligram stimu-gel, and an eight-ounce glass of soy milk for breakfast, just like every other Tuesday. She leaves the dishes in the sink for later, because the trains have been running a little early the past week or so. She dresses quickly, deciding that she can get by one more day without a shower, deciding to wear black stockings, instead of navy. And she's out the door and waiting for the elevator by seven twenty-two, her head already sizzling from the stimugel.

On the train, she stares out at the winter-gray landscape, Manhattan in mid-January, and listens to the CNN2 Firstlight report over the train's tinny speakers: the war in Turkey, the war in North Africa, the war in India, an ecoterrorist attack in Uruguay, Senate hearings on California's state-funded "suicide camps," the weather, the stock-market report, the untimely death of an actor she's never seen. The train races the clock across the Hudson and into Jersey, and, because it's Tuesday morning, the Firstlight anchorwoman reminds everyone that there will be no private operation of non-electric vehicles until Thursday morning at ten o'clock Eastern, ten o'clock Pacific.

The day unfolds around her in no way that is noticeably different from any other Tuesday.

Farasha eats her lunch (a chocolate-flavored protein bar and an apple from the vending machines) and is back at her desk three minutes before anyone else. At one nineteen, the network burps, and everyone in datatrak and receiving is advised to crossfile and reboot. At one minute past three, the fat guy five desks over from her laughs aloud to himself and is duly docked twelve points plus five percent for inattentive behavior. He glances nervously at the nearest observer, risking another citation, risking unemployment, and then goes back to work. At four thirty-eight, the lights on the fourth floor dim themselves for seven minutes, because it is Tuesday, and even the corporations are willing to make these inconvenient, necessary sacrifices in the interest of energy conservation. Good examples are set at the top, after all.

At six PM, as a light snow begins to fall, she walks alone with all the others to the Palisades station and takes the lev back across the river, back to the city. On the train, she watches the snow and the lights dotting the gathering night and listens indifferently to the CNN2 WindDown broadcast. The stimugel capsule is wearing off early, and she reminds herself to mention it to her physician next month. It wouldn't be the first time she's needed her dosage adjusted.

Farasha is home by seven thirty, and she changes clothes, trading the black stockings for bare legs, then eats her dinner—a spongy slice of vegetarian meatloaf with a few spoonfuls of green peas and carrots on the side, a stale wheat roll and a cup of hot, sweetened mint tea. The tea is good, at least, and she sips the last of it in front of the television, two black-and-white *Popeye the Sailor* cartoons and one in color with Tom and Jerry. Her company therapist recommended cartoons in the evening, and she enjoys them, though they don't seem to do anything for her insomnia or the nightmares. Her insurance would cover sleep mods and rem reconditioning, but she knows it's best not to make too much of the bad dreams. It's not something she wants on her record, not something she wants her supervisors getting curious about.

She shuts off the television at nine o'clock, does the dishes, takes the short, cold shower she's been putting off for three days, and then checks her mail before bed. There's something wordy and unimportant from her half sister in Montreal, an ad for breast enhancement that slipped through the spamblock, a reminder that city elections are only a month away and she's required by company policy to vote GOP, and something else that's probably only more spam. Farasha reads the vague header on the fourth item— INVITATION TRANSCEND—then tells the computer to empty the inbox. She touches the upper left-hand corner of the screen, an index finger pressed against and then into the phosphor triangle, and it vanishes. The wall above the kitchen counter is only a wall again.

She brushes her teeth, flosses, takes a piss, then washes her hands, and is in bed by nine forty-six. She falls asleep ten or twenty minutes later, trying not to think about the dreams, or the next day, concentrating on the steady roar of a water sweeper moving slowly, methodically along Mercer Street.

Farasha Kim was born in Trenton, the year before the beginning of the Pan-American/European Birth Lottery, to a Saudi mother and a Korean father. She was one of the last "freeborn" children in the US, though she doesn't see this as a point of pride. Farasha has never bothered with the lottery, not with the birth-defect rate what it is these days, and not when there are already more than ten billion people in the world, most of them living in conditions she prefers not contemplate. Her father, a molecular biochemist at Columbia University, has told her more than once that her own birth was an "accident" and "ill-timed," and she has no wish to repeat any of the mistakes of her parents.

She grew up in Lower Manhattan, suffering the impeccably programmed attentions of the nanny mechs that did the work her mother and father couldn't be bothered with. Sometimes in the uncomfortable dreams that wake her every night, Farasha is a child again. She's five, or eight, or even eleven, and there's usually a nagging sense of loss, of disappointment and sadness, when she wakes to discover herself aged to thirty-seven years.

In one recurring dream, repeated at least twice a month, she's eight and on a school field trip to the Museum of Modern Art. She stands with the edu-mechs and other children, all nameless in the fickle memory of her unconsciousness, gazing up at an enormous canvas hung on a wide white wall. There are no other paintings on the wall. A towering rectangle of pigment and cold-pressed linseed oil, sweeping arcs of color, a riot of blues and greens and pinks and violets. Sea foam and rising bubbles, the sandy, sun-dappled floor of a tropical lagoon, coral and giant clams and the teardrop bodies of fish. Positioned near the center is the figure of a woman, a *naked* woman, her skin almost the same shade of brown as Farasha's own, swimming towards the shimmering mirror surface. Her arms outstretched, air streaming from her wide nostrils and open mouth, her strong legs driving her up and up and up. And near the bottom of the painting, lurking in lower left-hand shadows, there's a shark with snow-tipped caudal and dorsal fins. It isn't clear whether or not the shark poses an immediate danger to the swimmer, but the *threat* is plain to see.

There's a label fixed to the wall beneath the painting, black lettering stark against all that white, so she knows it's titled "The Pearl Diver." No such painting has ever hung at MoMA; she's inquired more than once. She's also searched online databases and library hardcopies, but has found no evidence that the painting is anything but a fabrication of her dreaming mind. She's never mentioned it to her therapist, or to anyone else, for that matter.

In her dream, one of the children (never precisely the same child twice) asks one of the edu-mechs what the woman in the painting is doing, and the droid answers patiently, first explaining what pearls are, in case some of its students might not know.

"A natural pearl," the mech says, "forms by secretions from the epithelial cells in the mantle of some mollusks, such as oysters, deposited in successive layers about an irritating foreign object, often a parasitic organism. Layers of aragonite or calcite, the crystalline forms of calcium carbonate, accumulate..."

But the eight-year-old Farasha is always more interested in the painting itself, the brushstroke movement and color of the painting, than in the mere facts behind its subject matter, and she concentrates on the canvas while the mech talks. She tunes it out, and the other children, too, and the walls of the museum, and the marble floor beneath her feet.

She tastes the impossibly clean saltwater getting into her mouth, and her oxygen-starved lungs ache for air. Beneath her, the shark moves silently forward, a silver-blue-gray ghost propelled by the powerful side-to-side sweeps of its tall heterocercal tail. It knows things that she can only guess, things that she will never see, even in dreams.

Eventually, the droid finishes with all the twists and turns of its encyclopedia reply and ushers the other children towards the next painting in the gallery. But Farasha is left behind, unnoticed, forgotten, abandoned because she can no longer separate herself from "The Pearl Diver." Her face and hands are stained with paint, and she's still rising, struggling for the glistening surface that seems to be getting farther away, instead of nearer. She wonders if people can drown in paintings and kicks her legs again, going nowhere at all.

The shark's dull eyes roll back like the eyes of something dead or dying, and its jaws gape open wide to reveal the abyss waiting for her past the rows and rows of ragged teeth. Eternity in there, all the eternity she might ever have imagined or feared.

And the canvas pulls her in.

And sometimes she wakes up, and sometimes she drifts down through frost and darkness filled with anxious, whispering voices, and sometimes the dream architecture collapses and becomes another dream entirely.

There's a small plastic box on Farasha's bedroom dressing table, polyethylene terephthalate molded and colored to look like carved ivory, and inside are three perfect antique pearls from a broken strand that once belonged to one of her Arab great-grandmothers. Her mother gave her the pearls as a birthday present many years ago, and she's been told that they're worth a lot of money. The oyster species that produced them has been extinct for almost a thirty years. Sometimes, she goes to the dressing table after the dream and opens the plastic box, takes out one or two or all three of the pearls and carries them back to bed with her. In her sweating, sleepless palms, they feel very heavy, as good as stone or lead, and she can't imagine how anyone could have ever worn an entire necklace of them strung about her neck.

On those mornings after "The Pearl Diver," when it's finally six thirty-five, and the pillow has begun to bleat at her, Farasha gets up and returns the heirloom pearls to their box, which they share with the few inexpensive, unremarkable pieces of jewelry that she owns. She never takes the pearls out any other time, and she tries not to think about them. She would gladly forget them, would sell them off for whatever she could get, if it meant the dream would stop.

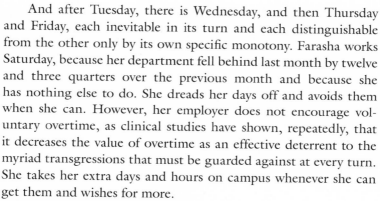

And after Tuesday, there is Wednesday, and then Thursday and Friday, each inevitable in its turn and each distinguishable from the other only by its own specific monotony. Farasha works Saturday, because her department fell behind last month by twelve and three quarters over the previous month and because she has nothing else to do. She dreads her days off and avoids them when she can. However, her employer does not encourage voluntary overtime, as clinical studies have shown, repeatedly, that it decreases the value of overtime as an effective deterrent to the myriad transgressions that must be guarded against at every turn. She takes her extra days and hours on campus whenever she can get them and wishes for more.

On Sunday, there is no work, and she isn't religious, so she doesn't go to church, either. Instead, she sits alone in her two-room apartment on Canal Street. The intermittent snow showers of the last four days have been replaced by a torrential rain which drums loudly against her window. For lunch, she has a can of cheese ravioli and a few slices of dried pear, then tries again to get interested in a romance fic she downloaded the weekend before. She sits in the comfortable chair beside her bed, the lines of text scrolling tediously by on portable, hidden sensors reading the motion of her eyes from word to word, sentence to sentence. When the computer detects her growing disinterest, it asks if she would prefer the fic be read aloud to her, and Farasha declines. She's never liked being read to by machines, though she can't recall ever having been read to by a human.

"My mail, please," she says, and the fic dissolves, becoming instead the inbox of her corporate account. There's a reminder for a planning meeting on Monday morning, a catalog from a pharmaceutical spa in Nevada, and another mail with the subject line INVITATION TRANSCEND. She starts to tell the computer to delete all three, even though it would probably mean a warning from interdept comms for failing to read an official memorandum. Instead, she taps the screen with the nail of her left index finger, tapping INVITATION TRANSCEND before she can think better of it. The portable advises her that all unsolicited mail, if read, is immediately noted and filed with the Homeland Bureau of Casual Correspondence and the Federal Bureau of Investigation and asks her if she still wishes to open the file. She tells it yes, and the blue and white HBCC/FBI notice is promptly replaced with the body of the message. She notes at once that the sender's address is not displayed, even though the portable is running the corporation's own custom version of MS Panoptic 8. Farasha shifts in the chair, and its legs squeak loudly against the tile floor, squeaking like the sleek, quick rats that infest the building's basement.

The message reads simply:

INVITATION TRANSCEND
Final [2nd] outreach imminent. Your presence is requested. Delivery complete and confidential [guaranteed]. There is meaning in you and Outside, still. You shall see that. Wholeness regained through communion with the immaculate appetite. One way. Sonepur. Baudh. Mahanadi. This overture will NOT be repeated. Open doors do not remain open forever, Ms. Kim. Please expect contact. Merciful closure. Shantih. Amen. Off.

"Bullshit," Farasha mutters, scanning the message once more and finding it even more opaque and ridiculous the second time through. Someone had obviously managed to hack the drop tank again, and this was his or her or its idea of a joke. "Delete all," she says, hearing the annoyance in her voice, wondering how long its been since she's sounded that way. Too late, she remembers the unread memorandum on Monday morning's meeting, and a second later the portable informs her that the inbox is now empty, and that a federal complaint has been filed on her behalf.

She stares at the screen for a long moment, at the omnipresent corporate logo and the blinking cursor floating just slightly left of center. Then Farasha requests a search, and when the computer asks her for parameters, she types in two unfamiliar words from the vanished INVITATION TRANSCEND message, "Sonepur" and "Mahanadi." She thought the latter looked Hindi and isn't surprised when it turns out to be a river in central and eastern India. And "Sonepur" is a city located at the confluence of the Mahanadi and Tel rivers in the eastern part of the Subarnapur district. Most of the recent articles on Sonepur concern repeated bioweapon attacks on the city by Pakistani-backed guerrilla forces six months earlier. There are rumors that the retroviral agent involved may have originated somewhere in China, and the loss of life is estimated to have been staggering; a general quarantine of Sonepur remains in effect, but few other details are available. The computer reminds Farasha that searches involving military interests will be noted and filed with the Greater Office of Homeland Security, the FBI, CIA, and Interpol.

She frowns and shuts off the portable, setting it down on the small bamboo table beside the bed. Tomorrow, she'll file an appeal on the search, citing the strange piece of mail as just cause. Her record is good, and there's nothing to worry about. Outside, the rain is coming down harder than ever, falling like it means to wash Manhattan clean or drown it trying, and she sits listening to the storm, wishing that she could have gone into work.

Monday again, after the morning's meeting, and Farasha is sitting at her desk. Someone whispers "Woolgathering?" and she turns her head to see who's spoken. But it's only Nadine Palmer, who occupies the first desk to her right. Nadine Palmer, who seems intent on ignoring company policy regarding unnecessary speech and who's likely to find herself unemployed if she keeps it up. Farasha knows better than to tempt the monitors by replying to the question. Instead, she glances down at the pad in front of her, the sloppy black lines her stylus has traced on the silver-blue screen, the two

Hindi words—"Sonepur" and "Mahanadi"—the city and the river, two words that have nothing whatsoever to do with the Nakamura-Ito account. She's scribbled them over and over, one after the other. Farasha wonders how long she's been sitting there daydreaming, and if anyone besides Nadine has noticed. She looks at the clock and sees that there's only ten minutes left before lunch, then clears the pad.

She stays at her desk through the lunch hour, to make up the twelve minutes she squandered "woolgathering." She isn't hungry, anyway.

At precisely two p.m., all the others come back from their midday meals, and Farasha notices that Nadine Palmer has a small stain that looks like ketchup on the front of her pink blouse.

At three twenty-four, Farasha completes her second post-analysis report of the day.

At four thirteen, she begins to wish that she hadn't found it necessary to skip lunch.

And at four fifty-six, she receives a voicecall informing her that she's to appear in Mr. Binder's office on the tenth floor no later than a quarter past five. Failure to comply will, of course, result in immediate dismissal and forfeiture of all unemployment benefits and references. Farasha thanks the very polite, yet very adamant, young man who made the call, then straightens her desk and shuts off her terminal before walking to the elevator. Her mouth has gone dry, and her heart is beating too fast. By the time the elevator doors slide open, opening for her like the jaws of an oil-paint shark, there's a knot deep in her belly, and she can feel the sweat beginning to bead on her forehead and upper lip. Mr. Binder's office has a rhododendron in a terra-cotta pot and a view of the river and the city beyond. "You are Ms. Kim?" he asks, not looking up from his desk. He's wearing a navy-blue suit with a teal necktie, and what's left of his hair is the color of milk.

"Yes sir."

"You've been with the company for a long time now, haven't you? It says here that you've been with us since college."

"Yes sir, I have."

"But you deleted an unread interdepartmental memorandum yesterday, didn't you?"

"That was an accident. I'd intended to read it."

"But you *didn't*."

"No sir," she replies, and glances at the rhododendron.

"May I ask what is your interest in India, Ms. Kim?" and at first she has no idea what he's talking about. Then she remembers the letter—INVITATION TRANSCEND—and her web search on the two words she'd caught herself doodling earlier in the day.

"None, sir. I can explain."

"I understand that there was an incident report filed yesterday evening with the GOHS, a report filed against you, Ms. Kim. Are you aware of that?"

"Yes sir. I'd meant to file an appeal this morning. It slipped my mind—"

"And what are your interests in India?" he asks her again and looks up, finally, and smiles an impatient smile at her.

"I have no interest in India, sir. I was just curious, that's all, because of a letter—"

"A letter?"

"Well, not really a letter. Not exactly. Just a piece of spam that got through—"

"Why would you read unsolicited mail?" he asks.

"I don't know. I can't say. It was the second time I'd received it, and—"

"Kim. Is that Chinese?"

"No, sir. It's Korean."

"Yes, of course it is. I trust you understand our position in this very delicate matter, Ms. Kim. We appreciate the work you've done here, I'm sure, and regret the necessity of this action, but we can't afford a federal investigation because one of our employees can't keep her curiosity in check."

"Yes, sir," Farasha says quietly, the knot in her stomach winding itself tighter as something icy that's not quite panic or despair washes over and through her. "I understand."

"Thank you, Ms. Kim. An agent will be in contact regarding your severance. Do not return to your desk. An officer will escort you off the campus."

And then it's over, five nineteen by the clock on Mr. Binder's wall, and she's led from the building by a silent woman with shiny, video-capture eyes, from the building and all the way back to the Palisades lev station, where the officer waits with her until the next train back to Manhattan arrives and she's aboard.

It's raining again by the time Farasha reaches Canal Street, a light, misting rain that'll probably turn to sleet before morning. She thinks about her umbrella, tucked beneath her desk as she waits for the security code to clear and the lobby door to open. *No*, she thinks. *By now they'll have gotten rid of it. By now, they'll have cleared away any evidence I was ever there.*

She takes the stairs, enough of elevators for one day, and by the time she reaches her floor, she's breathless and a little light-headed. There's a faintly metallic taste in her mouth, and she looks back down the stairwell, picturing her body lying limp and broken at the very bottom.

"I'm not a coward," she says aloud, her voice echoing between the concrete walls, and then Farasha closes the red door marked EXIT and walks quickly down the long, fluorescent-lit hallway to her apartment. At least, it's hers until the tenant committee gets wind of her dismissal, of the reasons *behind* her dismissal, and files a petition for her relocation with the housing authority.

Someone has left a large manila envelope lying on the floor in front of her door. She starts to bend over to pick it up, then stops and glances back towards the door to the stairs, looks both ways, up and down the hall, to be sure that she's alone. She briefly considers pressing #0 on the keypad and letting someone in the lobby deal with this. She knows it doesn't matter if there's no one else in the hallway to see her pick up the envelope, because the cameras will record it.

"Fuck it all," she says, reaching for the envelope. "They can't very well fire me twice."

There's a lot left they can do, she thinks, some mean splinter of her that's still concerned with the possibility of things getting worse. *You don't even want to know all the things left they can do to you.*

Farasha picks up the envelope, anyway.

Her name has been handwritten on the front, printed in black ink, neat, blocky letters at least an inch high, and beneath her name, in somewhat smaller lettering, are two words—INVITATION TRANSCEND. The envelope is heavier than she expected, something more substantial inside than paper; she taps her code into the keypad, and the front door buzzes loudly and pops open. Farasha takes a moment to reset the lock's eight-digit code, violating the terms of her lease

—as well as one municipal and two federal ordinances—then takes the envelope to the kitchen counter.

Inside the manila envelope there are a number of things, which she spreads out across the countertop, then examines one by one. There's a single yellowed page torn from an old book; the paper is brittle, and there's no indication what the book might have been. The top of the page bears the header *Childhood of the Human Hero,* so perhaps that was the title. At the bottom is a page number, 327, and the following paragraph has been marked with a blue highlighter:

> *The feats of the beloved Hindu savior, Krishna, during his infant exile among the cowherds of Gokula and Brindaban, constitute a lively cycle. A certain goblin named Putana came in the shape of a beautiful woman, but with poison in her breasts. She entered the house of Yasoda, the foster mother of the child, and made herself very*

friendly, presently taking the baby in her lap to give it suck. But Krishna drew so hard that he sucked away her life, and she fell dead, reassuming her huge and hideous form. When the foul corpse was cremated, however, it emitted a sweet fragrance; for the divine infant had given the demoness salvation when he had drunk her milk.

At the bottom of the page, written with a pencil in very neat, precise cursive, are three lines Farasha recognizes from T. S. Eliot: *And I will show you something different from either/Your shadow @ morning striding behind you/Or your shadow @ evening rising up to meet you.*

There are three newspaper clippings, held together with a somewhat rusty gem clip, all regarding the use of biological agents by pro-Pakistani forces in Sonepur and Baudh (which turns out to be another city on the Mahanadi River). More than three million are believed dead, one article states, though the quarantine has made an accurate death toll impossible, and the final number may prove to be many times that. Both the CDC and WHO have been refused entry into the contaminated areas, and the nature of the contagion remains unclear. There are rumors of vast fires burning out of control along the river, and of mass disappearances in neighboring towns, and she reads the names of Sikh and Assamese rebel leaders who have been detained or executed.

There is a stoppered glass vial containing what looks to Farasha like soot, perhaps half a gram of the black powder, and the vial is sealed with a bit of orange tape.

There is a photocopy of an eight-year-old NASA press release on the chemical composition of water-ice samples recovered from the lunar South Pole, and another on the presence of "polycyclic aromatic hydrocarbons, oxidized sulfide compounds, and carbonate globules" in a meteorite discovered embedded in the Middle Devonian-aged rocks of Antarctica's Mt. Gudmundson in July 2037.

Finally, there's the item which gave the envelope its unexpected weight, a silvery metallic disk about ten centimeters in diameter and at least two centimeters thick. Its edges are beveled and marked by a deep groove, and there is a pronounced dimple in the center of one side, matching a swelling at the center of the other. The metal is oddly warm to the touch, and though it seems soft, almost pliant in her hands, when Farasha tries to scratch it with a steak knife, she's unable to leave even the faintest mark.

She glances at the clock on the wall above the refrigerator and realizes that more than two hours have passed since she sat down with the envelope, that she has no sense of so much time having passed unnoticed, and the realization makes her uneasy. *I have slipped and fallen off the earth,* she thinks, remembering Mr. Binder's potted rhododendron. *Not even time can find me now.* And then she looks back at the contents of the manila envelope.

"Is it a riddle?" she asks aloud, asking no one or herself or whoever left the package at her doorstep. "Am I supposed to understand any of this?"

For an answer, her stomach growls loudly, and Farasha glances at the clock again, adding up all the long hours since breakfast. She leaves the papers, the glass vial, the peculiar metal disk, the empty envelope—all of it—lying on the countertop and makes herself a cheddar-cheese sandwich with brown mustard. She pours a glass of soy milk and sits down on the kitchen floor. *Even unemployed ghosts have to eat,* she thinks, and laughs softly to herself. *Even dead women drifting alone in space get hungry, now and then.*

When she's finished, she sets the dirty dishes in the sink and goes back to her stool at the counter, back to pondering the things from the envelope. Outside, the rain has turned to sleet, just as she suspected it would, and it crackles coldly against the windows.

The child reaches out her hand, straining to touch the painting, and her fingertips dip into salty, cool water. Her lips part, and air escapes through the space between her teeth and floats in swirling, glassy bubbles towards the surface of the sea. She kicks her feet, and the shark's sandpaper skin slices through the gloom, making a sound like metal scraping stone. If she looked down, towards the sandy place where giant clams lie in secret, coral- and anemone-encrusted gardens, she'd see sparks fly as the great fish cuts its way towards her. The sea is not her protector and isn't taking sides. She came to steal, after all, and the shark is only doing what sharks have done for the last four hundred and fifty million years. It's nothing personal, nothing she hasn't been expecting.

The child cries out and pulls her hand back; her fingers are stained with paint and smell faintly of low tide and turpentine.

The river's burning, and the night sky is the color of an apocalypse. White temples of weathered stone rise from the whispering jungles, ancient monuments to alien gods—Shiva, Parvati, Kartikeya, Brushava, Ganesha—crumbling prayers to pale blue skins and borrowed tusks.

Farasha looks at the sky, and the stars have begun to fall, drawing momentary lines of clean white fire through the billowing smoke. Heaven will intercede, and this ruined world will pass away and rise anew from its own gray ashes. A helicopter drifts above the bloody river like a great insect of steel and spinning rotors, and she closes her eyes before it sees her.

"I was never any good with riddles," she says, when Mr. Binder asks her about the package again, why she touched it, why she opened it, why she read all the things inside.

"It isn't a riddle," he scolds, and his voice is thunder and waves breaking against rocky shores and wind through the trees. "It's a gift."

"I was never any good with gifts, either," she replies, watching as the glass vial from the manila envelope slips from his fingers and begins the long descent towards her kitchen floor. It might fall for a hundred years, for a hundred *thousand* years, but she'll never be quick enough to catch it.

The child reaches deep into the painting again, deeper than before, and now the water has gone as cold as ice and burns her hand. She grits her teeth against the pain, and feels the shark brush past her frozen skin.

"If it's not already within you, no one can put it there," the droid says to her as it begins to unbutton the pink, ketchup-stained blouse she doesn't remember putting on. "We have no wombs but those which open for us."

"I told you, I'm not any good with riddles."

Farasha is standing naked in her kitchen, bathed in the light of falling stars and burning rivers and the fluorescent tubes set into the low ceiling. There's a girl in a rumpled school uniform standing nearby, her back turned to Farasha, watching the vial from the envelope as it tumbles end over end towards the floor. The child's hands and forearms are smeared with greasy shades of cobalt and jade and hyacinth.

"You have neither love, nor the hope of love," the girl says. "You have neither purpose, nor a dream of purpose. You have neither pain, nor freedom from pain." Then she turns her head, looking over her right shoulder at Farasha. "You don't even have a job."

"Did you do that? You *did*, didn't you?"

"You opened the envelope," the child says and smiles knowingly, then turns back to the falling vial. "You're the one who read the message."

The shark is coming for her, an engine of blood and cartilage, dentine and bone, an engine forged and perfected without love or the hope of love, without purpose or freedom from pain. The air in her lungs expands as she rises, and her exhausted, unperfect primate muscles have begun to ache and cramp. *This is not your world,* the shark growls, and she's not surprised that it has her mother's voice. *You gave all this shit up aeons ago. You crawled out into the slime and the sun looking for God, remember?*

"It was an invitation, that's all," the girl says and shrugs. The vial is only a few inches from the floor now. "You're free to turn us away. There will always be others."

"I don't understand what you're *saying*," Farasha tells the girl and then takes a step back, anticipating the moment when the vial finally strikes the hard tile floor.

"Then stop trying."

"Sonepur—"

"That wasn't our doing," the girl says and shakes her head. "A *man* did that. Men would make a weapon of the entire cosmos, given enough time."

"I don't know what you're offering me."

The girl turns to face Farasha, holding out one paint-stained hand. There are three pearls resting in her palm.

The jungle echoes with rifle and machinegun fire and the dull violence of faraway explosions. The muddy, crooked path that Farasha has taken from the river bank ends at the steps of a great temple, and the air here is choked with the sugary scent of night-blooming flowers, bright and corpulent blooms that almost manage to hide the riper stink of dead things.

"But from out your *own* flesh," the girl says, her eyes throwing sparks now, like the shark rushing towards her. "The fruit of *your* suffering, Farasha Kim, not these inconsequential baubles—"

"I'm *afraid*," Farasha whispers, not wanting to cry, and she begins to climb the temple steps, taking them cautiously, one at a time. The vial from the envelope shatters, scattering the sooty black powder across her kitchen floor.

"That's why I'm here," the child says and smiles again. She makes a fist, closing her hand tightly around the three pearls as a vertical slit appears in the space between Farasha's bare breasts, its edges red and puckered like a slowly healing wound. The slit opens wide to accept the child's seeds.

The pain Farasha feels is not so very different from the pain she's felt her entire life.

Farasha opens her eyes, in the not-quite-empty moments left after the dream, and she squints at the silver disk from the manila envelope. It's hovering a couple of inches above the countertop, spinning clockwise and emitting a low, mechanical whine. A razor-thin beam of light leaks from the dimple on the side facing upwards, light the lonely color of a winter sky before heavy snow. The beam is slightly wider where it meets the ceiling than where it exits the disk, and the air smells like ozone. She rubs her eyes and sits up. Her back pops, and her neck is stiff from falling asleep at the kitchen counter. Her mouth is dry and tastes vaguely of the things she ate for her supper.

She glances from the spinning disk to the glass vial, still stoppered and sealed with a strip of orange tape, and her left hand goes slowly to the space between her breasts. Farasha presses three fingers against the thin barrier of cloth and muscle and skin covering her sternum, half-expecting something on the other side to press back. But there's nothing, nothing at all except the faint rhythm of her heart, and she reaches for the vial. Her hand is shaking, and it rolls away from her and disappears over the far edge of the counter. A second or two later, there's the sound of breaking glass.

The disk is spinning faster now, and the light shining from the dimple turns a bruised violet.

She looks down at the scatter of paper, and her eyes settle on the three handwritten lines from *The Waste Land*. She reads them aloud, and they feel wild and irrevocable on her tongue, poetry become the components of an alchemical rite or the constituent symbols in some algebraic equation. *And I will show you something different from either/Your shadow at morning striding behind you/Or your shadow at evening rising up to meet you.* Nine, seven, ten, dividing into thirty-eight syllables, one hundred and nineteen characters.

But what if I won't listen? she thinks. *What if I won't see?* And she's answered at once by the voice of a child, the voice of a brown woman who dives for gems in a painted ocean, the wordless voice of the sooty particles from the broken vial as they fill the air Farasha's breathing and find their way deep inside her.

That's why I'm here, remember? the voices reply, almost speaking in unison now, a secret choir struggling for harmony, and the disk on the counter stops suddenly and then begins to spin in the opposite direction. The beam of light has turned a garish scarlet, and it pulsates in time to her racing heart. The contagion is faster than she ever could have imagined, and this is not the pain from her dream. This is pain doubled and redoubled, pain become something infinitely greater than mere electrical impulses passed between neurons and the folds of her simple, mammalian brain. But Farasha understands, finally, and she doesn't struggle as the soot begins its work of taking her apart and putting her back together another way, dividing polypeptide chains and inserting its own particular amino acids before it zips them shut again.

And her stolen body, like the fractured, ephemeral landscape of her nightmares, becomes something infinitely mutable, altered from second to second to second, living tissue as malleable as paint on a bare canvas. There is not death here, and there is no longer loneliness or fear, boredom or the dread of whatever's coming next. With eyes that have never truly seen before this moment, Farasha watches at her soul fills up with pearls.

In View of Nothing

Oh, pity us here, we angels of lead.
We're dead, we're sick, hanging by thread...
David Bowie ("Get Real," 1995)

02. The Bed

M y breasts ache.
I have enough trouble just remembering the name of this city, and I have yet to be convinced that the name remains the same from one day to the next, one night to the next night. Or that the city itself remains the same. These are the very sorts of details that will be my undoing someday, someday quite soon, if I am anything less than mindful. Today, I believe that I have awakened in Sakyo-ku, in the Kyoto Prefecture, but lying here staring up at the bright banks of fluorescent lights on the ceiling, I might be anywhere. I might well be in Boston or Johannesburg or Sydney, and maybe I've never even been to Japan. Maybe I have lived my entire life without setting foot in Kyoto.

From where I lie, almost everything seems merely various shades of unwelcome conjecture. Almost everything. I think about getting up and going to the window, because from there I might confirm or deny my Kyoto hypothesis. I might spy the Kamo River, flowing down from its source on Mount Sajikigatake, or the withered cherry trees that did not blossom last year and perhaps will not blossom this spring, either. I might see the silver-grey ribbon of the Kamo, running between the neon-scarlet flicker of torii gates at the Kamigamo and Shimogamo shrines.

Maybe that window looks eastward, towards the not-so-distant ocean, and I would see Mount Daimonji. Or I might see only the steel and glass wall of a neighboring skyscraper.

I lie where I am and do not go to the window, and I stare up at the low plaster ceiling, the ugly water stains spread out there like bruises or melanoma or concentric geographical features on an ice moon of Saturn or Jupiter or Neptune. This whole goddamn building is rotten; I recall that much clearly enough. The ceiling of my room—if it *is* my room—has more leaks than I can count, and it's not even on the top floor. The rain is loud against the window, but the dripping ceiling seems to my ears much louder, as each drop grows finally too heavy and falls to the ceramic tiles. I hear a distinct *plink* for each and every drop that drips down from the motel ceiling, and that *plink* does not quite seem to match what I recall about the sound of water dripping against tile.

The paler-than-oyster sheets are damp, too. As are the mattress and box springs underneath. Why there are not mushrooms, I can't say. There is mold, mold or mildew if there's some difference between the two, because I can smell it, and I can see it.

I lie here on my back and stare up at the leaky ceiling, listening to the rain, letting these vague thoughts ricochet through my incontinent skull. My mind leaks, too, I suspect, and in much the same way that this ceiling leaks. My thoughts and memories have stained the moldering sheets, discrete units of me drifting away in a slow flood of cerebrospinal fluid, my ears for sluice gates— or my eyes—*Liquor cerebrospinalis* draining out a few precious milliliters per day or hour, leaving only vast echoes in emptied subarachnoid cavities.

She looks at me over her left shoulder, her skin as white as snow that never falls, her hair whiter still, her eyes like broken sapphire shards, and she frowns, knitting her white eyebrows. She is talking into the antique black rotary telephone, but looking at me, disapproving of these meandering, senseless thoughts when I have yet to answer her questions to anyone's satisfaction. I turn away—the exact wrong thing to do, and yet I do it, anyway. I wish she would put some clothes on. Her robe is hanging on a hook not far away. I would get it for her, if she would only ask. She lights a cigarette, and that's good, because now the air wrapped all about the bed smells less like the mold and poisonous rainwater.

"We do the best we can," she tells the telephone, whoever's listening on the other end of the line, "given what we have to work with."

Having turned away, I lie on my left side, my face pressing into those damp sheets, shivering and wondering how long now since I have been genuinely warm. Wondering, too, if this season is spring or winter or autumn. I am fairly certain it is not summer. She laughs, but I don't shut my eyes. I imagine that the folds and creases of the sheets are ridges and valleys, and I am the slain giant of some creation myth. My cerebrospinal fluid will form lakes and rivers and seas, and trees will sprout, and grass and ferns and lichen, and all that vegetation shall be imbued with my lost or merely forfeited memories. The birds will rise up from fancies that have bled from me.

My breasts ache.

Maybe that has some role to play in this cosmogony, the aching, swollen breasts of the fallen giantess whose mind became the wide white-grey world.

"I need more time, that's all," the naked snow-coloured woman tells the black Bakelite handset. "There were so many more layers than we'd anticipated."

With an index finger I trace the course of one of the V-shaped sheet valleys. It gradually widens towards the foot of the bed, towards my *own* feet, and I decide that I shall arbitrarily call that direction *south*, as I arbitrarily think this motel might exist somewhere in Kyoto. Where it ends, there is a broad alluvial fan, this silk-cotton blend splaying out into flat deltas where an unseen river at last deposits its burden of mnemonic silt and clay and sand— only the finest particles make it all the way over the far away edge of the bed to the white-tile sea spread out below. Never meaning to, I have made a *flat* white-grey world. Beyond the delta are low hills, smooth ridges in the shadow of my knees. Call it an eclipse, that gloom; *any* shadow in this stark room is Divine.

These thoughts are leading me nowhere, and I think now that they must exist only to erect a defence, this complete absence of direction. She has pried and stabbed and pricked that fragile innermost stratum of the meningeal envelope, the precious pia matter, and so triggered inside me these meandering responses. She thought to find only pliable grey matter waiting underneath, and maybe the answers to her questions—tap in, cross ref, download—but, no, here's this damned firewall, instead. But I did not put it there. I am holding nothing back by choice. I know she won't believe that, though it is the truth.

"Maybe another twelve hours," she tells the handset.

I must be a barren, pitiless goddess, to have placed all those fluorescent tubes for a sun and nothing else. They shed no warmth from out that otherwise starless ivory firmament. Heaven drips to make a filthy sea, and she rings off and places the handset back into its Bakelite cradle. It is all a cradle, I think, this room in this motel in this city I cannot name with any certainty. Perhaps I never even left Manhattan or Atlanta or San Francisco.

"I'm losing patience," she says and sighs impatiently. "More importantly, they're losing patience with me."

And I apologise again, though I am not actually certain this statement warrants an apology. I turn my head and watch as she leans back against her pillow, lifting the stumps of her legs onto the bed. She once told me how she lost them, and it was not so very long ago when she told me, but I can no longer remember that, either.

She smokes her cigarette, and her blue eyes seem fixed on something beyond the walls of the motel room.

"Maybe I should look at the book again," I suggest.

"Maybe," she agrees. "Or maybe I should put a bullet in your skull and say it was an accident."

"Or that I was trying to escape."

She nods and takes another drag off her cigarette. "If you are a goddess," she asks, "what the fuck does that make me?"

But I have no response for that. No response whatsoever. The smoke from her lips and nostrils hangs above our damp bed like the first clouds spreading out above my flat creation of sheets and fallen giants. Her skin is milk, and my breasts ache.

I close my eyes, and possibly I smell cherry blossoms behind her smoke and the stink of mildew, and I try hard to recollect when I first walked the avenues of Kyoto's Good Luck Meadow—Yoshiwara—the green houses and courtesans, boy whores and tea-shop girls, kabuki and paper dragons.

"You have never left this room," she tells me, and I have no compelling reason to believe her or to suspect that she's lying.

"We could shut off the lights," I say. "It could be dark for a little while."

"There isn't time now," she replies and stubs out her cigarette on the wall beside the bed, then drops the butt to the floor, and I think I hear a very faint hiss when it hits the damp tiles. She's left an ashen smudge on the wall near the plastic headboard, and that, I think, must be how evil enters the world.

04. The Book (1)

This is the very first time that she will show me the scrapbook. I *call* it a scrapbook, because I don't know what else to call it. Her robotic knees whir and click softly as she leans forward and snaps open the leather attaché case. She takes the scrapbook out and sets it on the counter beside the rust-streaked sink. This is an hour or so after the first time we made love, and I'm still in bed, watching her and thinking how much more beautiful she is without the ungainly chromium-plated prosthetics. The skin around the external fix posts and neural ports is pink and inflamed, and I wonder if she even bothers to keep them clean. I wonder how much it must hurt, being hauled about by those contraptions. She closes the lid of the briefcase, her every move deliberate, somehow calculated without seeming stiff, and the ankle joints purr like a tick-tock cat as she turns towards me. She is still naked, and I marvel again at the pallid thatch of her pubic hair. She retrieves the scrapbook from the sink.

"You look at the photographs," she says, "and tell me what you see there. This is what matters now, your impressions. We know the rest already."

"I need a hot shower," I tell her, but she shakes her head, and the robotic legs whir and move her towards the bed on broad tridactyl feet.

"Later," she says. "Later, you can have a hot shower, after we're done here."

And so I take the scrapbook from her when she offers it to me—a thick sheaf of yellowed pages held between two sturdy brown pieces of cardstock, and the whole thing bound together with a length of brown string. The strings have been laced through perforations in the pages and through small silver grommets set into the cardstock covers, and each end of the string is finished with black aiglets to keep it from fraying. The string has been tied into a sloppy sort of reef knot. There is nothing printed or written on the cover.

"Open it," she says, and her prosthetics whine and hiss pneumatic laments as she sits down on the bed near me. The box springs creak.

"What am I supposed to see?" I ask her.

"You are not *supposed* to see anything."

I open the scrapbook, and inside each page displays four black and white photographs, held in place by black metal photo corners. And at once I see, as it is plainly obvious, that all the photographs in the book are of the same man. Page after page after page, the same man, though not always the same photograph. They look like mug shots. The man is Caucasian, maybe forty-five years old, maybe fifty. His eyes are dark, and always he is staring directly into the camera lens. There are deep creases in his forehead, and his skin is mottled, large-pored, pockmarked. His lips are very thin, and his nose large and hooked. There are bags beneath his eyes.

"Who is he?" I ask.

"That's not your problem," she replies. "Just look at the pictures and tell me what you see."

I turn another page, and another, and another after that, and on every one that haggard face glares back at up me. "They're all the same."

"They are not," she says.

"I mean, they're all of the same man. Who is he?"

"I said that's not your problem. And surely you must know I haven't brought you here to tell me what I can see for myself."

So, I want to ask *why* she has brought me here, only I cannot recall *being* brought here. I am not certain I can recall anything before this white dripping room. It seems in this moment to be all I have ever known. I turn more pages, some so brittle they flake at my touch. But there is nothing to see here but the man with the shaved head and the hooked nose.

"Take your time," she says and lights another cigarette. "Just don't take too much of it."

"If this is about the syringes—"

"This isn't about the syringes. But we'll come to that later, trust me. And that Taiwanese chap, too, the lieutenant. What's his name?"

"The war isn't going well, is it?" I ask her, and now I look up from the scrapbook lying open in my lap and watch the darkness filling the doorway to our room. Our room or her room or my room, I cannot say which. That darkness seems as sticky and solid as hot asphalt.

"That depends whose side you're on," she says and smiles and flicks ash onto the floor.

It occurs to me for the first time that someone might be watching from that darkness, getting everything on tape, making notes, waiting and biding their time. I think I might well go mad if I stare too long into that impenetrable black. I look back down at the book, trying to see whatever it is she wants me to see on those pages, whatever it is she needs to know.

03. The Dream

The night after I lost the girl who lost the syringe—if any of that did in fact occur—I awoke in the white room on the not-quite-oyster sheets, gasping and squinting at those bare fluorescent tubes. My mouth so dry, my chest hurting, and the dream already beginning to fade. There was a pencil and a legal pad on the table beside the bed, and I wrote this much down:

This must have been near the end of it all, just before I finally woke. Being on the street of an Asian city, maybe Tokyo, I don't know. Night. Flickering neon and cosplay girls and noodle shops. The commingled smells of car exhaust and cooking and garbage. And I'm late for an appointment in a building I can see, an immaculate tower of shimmering steel. I can't read any of the street signs, because they're all Japanese or Mandarin or whatever. I'm lost. Men mutter as they pass me. The cosplay girls laugh and point. There's an immense animatronic Ganesh-like thing directing traffic (and I suppose this is foreshadowing). I finally find someone who doesn't speak English but she speaks German, and she shows me where to cross the street to reach the steel tower.

There might have been a lobby and an elevator ride, or I may only be filling in a jump cut. But then I was in the examination room of what seemed to be something very like a dentist's office. Only there wasn't that dentist-office smell. There was some other smell that only added to my unease and disorientation. I was asked to have a seat, please, in this thing that wasn't quite a dentist's chair. There was a woman with a British accent asking me questions, checking off items on a form of some sort.

She kept asking questions about my memory, and if I was comfortable. And then the woman with the British accent placed her thumb beneath my jaw, and I began to feel cold and fevery. She said something like, *We'll be as gentle as we can.* That's when

I saw that she was holding my jaw in her hands. And I could see my tongue and teeth and gums and lower lip and everything else. The sensation of cold grew more intense, and she told me to please remain calm, that it would all be over soon. Then she pressed something like a dental drill to my forehead, and there was a horrible whine and a burring sort of pain. She set the drill aside and plugged a jack into the roof of my mouth, something attached to an assortment of coaxial cables, and there was a suffocating blackness that seemed to rush up all around me.

I stare for a few moments at what I've written, then return the pencil and the pad to the table. My mouth tastes like onions and curry and aluminum foil, a metallic tang like a freshly filled molar, and I lie back down and shut my eyes tightly, wondering if the throbbing in my chest is the beginning of a heart attack or only indigestion. I'm sick to my stomach and dizzy, and I know that lying down and closing my eyes is the worst thing I could do for either. But I cannot bear the white glare of those bulbs. I will vomit, or it will pass without my having vomited, but I won't look up into that cold light. I do not know where I am or how I got here. I cannot recall ever having seen this dingy room before. No, not dingy—squalid. The sound of dripping water is very loud, a leaky ceiling, so at least maybe the damp sheets do not mean that I've pissed myself in my sleep. I lie very still, listening to the dripping water and to my pounding heart and to a restless sound that might be automobiles on the street outside.

05. The White Woman

She leans close, and her lips brush the lobe of my right ear, her tepid breath on my cheek, breath that smells of tobacco and more faintly of Indian cooking (cardamom, tamarind, fenugreek, cloves). She whispers, and her voice is *so* soft, so soft that she might in this moment have become someone else entirely.

"Nothing to be desired anymore," she whispers. "*Nichts gewünscht zu werden.*"

I don't argue. In this place and time, these are somehow words of kindness, words of absolution, and within them seems to rest the vague hope of release. Her body is warm against mine, her flat belly pressed against mine which is not so flat as it once was, her strong thighs laid against my thighs and her small breasts against my breasts. Together, we have formed an improbable binary opposition, lovers drawn from a deck of cards, my skin so pink and raw and hers so chalky and fine.

"*Gelassen gehen Sie,*" she whispers, and I open my eyes and gaze up into hers, those dazzling, broken blue gems. Her beauty is unearthly, and I might almost believe her an exile from another galaxy, a fallen angel, the calculated product of biotech and genetic alchemy. She lifts herself, rising up on those muscular arms, my hips seized firmly and held fast between the stumps of her transfemoral amputations. There was an accident when she was only a child, but that's all I can now recall. *This is how a mouse must feel,* I think, *in the claws of a cat, or a mouse lost in a laboratory maze.* She smiles, and that expression could mean so many different things.

She leans down again and kisses me, her tongue sliding easily between my teeth.

The room is filled with music, which I am almost certain wasn't there only a moment before. The scratchy, brittle tones of a phonograph recording, something to listen to besides the goddamn rain and the leaking ceiling and the creaking bed springs. And then she enters me, and it comes as no surprise that the robotic legs are not the full extent of her prosthetics. She slips her left arm beneath me, pulling me towards her, and I arch my back, finding her rhythm and the more predictable rhythm of the mechanical cock working its way deeper inside me.

In all the universe, there might be nothing but this room. In all the world, there might only be the two of us.

She kisses me again, but this time it is not a gentle act. This time, there is force and a violence only half-repressed, and I think of cats again. I do not want to think of cats, but I do. She will suck my breath, will draw my soul from me through my nostrils and lips to get at whatever it is she needs to know. How many souls would a woman like her have swallowed in her lifetime? She must be filled with ghosts, a gypsum alabaster bottle stoppered with two blue stones—lapis lazuli or chalcedony—cleverly shaped to resemble the eyes of a woman and not a cat and not an alabaster bottle filled with devoured souls.

Our lips part, and if she has taken my soul, it's nothing I ever needed anyway.

My mouth wanders across the smooth expanse above and between her breasts, and then I find her right nipple, and my tongue traces a mandala three times about her areola. Perhaps I have sorceries all my own.

"No, you don't," she says and thrusts her hips hard against mine.

And maybe I remember something then, so maybe this room is not all there is in all the world. Maybe I recall a train rushing along through long darknesses and brief puddles of mercury-vapour light, barreling forward, floating on old maglev tracks, and all around me are the cement walls of a narrow tunnel carved out deep below a city whose name I *cannot* recollect. But cities might not have names—I presently have no evidence that they do—and so perhaps this is not forgetfulness or amnesia, exactly. I turn my head and look out the window as the train races past a ruined and deserted station. I'm gripping a semi-automatic the way some women would hold onto a rosary or a string of tasbih beads. My forefinger slips through the familiar ring of the trigger guard...

"You still with me, sister?" the albino woman asks, and I nod as the memory of the train and the gun dissolves and is forgotten once again. I am sweating now, even in this cold, dank room on these sodden not-quite-oyster sheets, I am sweating. I could not say if it is from fear or exertion or from something else entirely.

And she comes then, her head bending back so far I think her neck will snap, the taut V of her clavicles below her delicate throat, and if only I had the teeth to do the job. She comes with a shudder and a gasp and a sudden rush of profanity in some odd, staccato language that I do not speak, have never even heard before, but still I know that those words are profane. I see that she is sweating, too, brilliant drops standing out like nectar on her too-white skin, and I lick away a salty trickle from her chest. So there's another way that she is in me now. Her body shudders again, and she releases me, withdrawing and rolling away to lie on her back. She is breathing heavily and grinning, and it is a perfectly merciless sort of grin, choked with triumph and bitter guile. I envy her that grin and the callous heart in back of it. Then my eyes go to that space between her legs, that fine white thatch of hair, and for a moment I only imagine the instrument of my seduction was *not* a prosthesis. For a moment, I watch the writhing, opalescent thing, still glistening and slick with me. Its body bristles with an assortment of fleshy spines, and I cannot help but ponder what venoms or exotic nanorobotic or nubot serums they might contain.

"Only a fleeting trick of the light, my love," she says, still grinning that brutal grin of hers. And I blink, and now there is only a dildo there between her legs, four or five inches of beige silicone molded into an erect phallus. I close my eyes again, and listen to the music and the rain tapping against the window.

01. The Train

The girl is sitting across the aisle and only three rows in front of me, and there's almost no one else riding the tube this late, just a very old man reading a paperback novel. But he's seated far away, many rows ahead of us, and only has eyes for his book, which he holds bent double in trembling, liver-spotted hands. The girl is wearing a raincoat made of lavender vinyl, the collar turned up high, so it's hard for me to get a good look at her face. Her hair is long and black and oily, and her hands are hidden inside snug leather gloves that match her raincoat. She's younger than I expected, maybe somewhere in her early twenties, maybe younger still, and a few years ago that might have made what I have to do next a lot harder. But running wet dispatch for the Greeks, you get numb to this sort of shit quick or you get into some other line of work. It doesn't matter how old she is, or that she might still have a mother and a father somewhere who love her, sisters or brothers, or that skimming parcels is the only thing keeping her from a life of whoring or selling herself off bit by bit to the carrion apes. These are most emphatically not my troubles. And soon, they will no longer be hers, either.

I glance back down the aisle towards the geezer, but he's still lost in the pages of his paperback.

The girl in the lavender coat is carrying, concealed somewhere on her person, seven 3/10ths cc syringes, and if I'm real goddamn fortunate, I'll never find out what's in them. It is not my job to know. It is my job to retrieve the package with as little fuss and fanfare and bloodshed as possible and then get it back across the border to the spooks in Alexandroupoli.

She wipes at her nose and then stares out the window at the tube walls hidden in the darkness.

I take a deep breath and glance back towards the old man. He hasn't moved a muscle, unless it's been to flip a page or two.

Mister, I think, *you just stay absolutely goddamn still, and maybe you'll get to find out how it ends.*

Then I check my gun again, to be double fucking sure the safety's off. With any sort of half-assed luck, I won't need the M9 tonight, but you live by better safe than sorry—if you live at all. The girl wipes her nose a second time and sniffles. Then she leans forward, resting her forehead against the back of the seat in front of her.

There's no time left to worry about whether or not the surveillance wasps are still running, taking it all in from their not-so-secret nooks and crannies, taking it all down. Another six minutes and we'll be pulling into the next terminal, and I have no intention of chasing this bitch in her lavender mack all over Ankara.

I stand and move quickly down the aisle towards her, flexing my left wrist to extend the niobium barb implanted beneath my skin. The neurotoxin will stop her heart before she even feels the prick, or so they tell me. Point is, she won't make a sound. It'll look like a heart attack, if anyone bothers with an autopsy, which I suspect they won't. I've been up against the Turks enough times now to know they only recruit the sort no one's ever going to miss anyway.

But then she turns and looks directly at me, and I've never seen eyes so blue. Or I've never seen eyes that *shade* of blue. Eyes that are both so terribly empty and so filled to bursting, and I know that something's gone very, very goddamn wrong. I know someone somewhere's lied to me, and this isn't just some kid plucked from the slums to mule pilfered load. She sits there, staring up at me, and I reach for the 9mm, shit-sure that's exactly the wrong thing to do, knowing that I've panicked even if I can't quite fathom *why* I've panicked. I'm close enough to get her with the barb, though now there might be a struggle, and then I'd have to deal with the old bookworm up front. I've hesitated, allowed myself to be distracted, and there's no way it's not gonna go down messy.

She smiles, a voracious, carnivorous smile.

"Nothing to be desired anymore," she says, and I feel the muscles in my hand and wrist relax, feel the barb retracting. I feel the gun slip from my slack fingers and hear it clatter to the floor.

"Go back to your seat," she tells me, but I've fallen so far into those eyes—those eyes that lead straight down through endless electric blue chasms, and I almost don't understand what she means. She leans over and picks my gun up off the floor of the maglev and hands it back to me.

"Go back to your seat," she says again, and I do. I turn and go back to my seat, returning the M9 to its shoulder holster, and sit staring at my hands or staring out the train window for what seems hours and hours and hours…

06. Marlene Dietrich

I sit alone at the foot of the bed, "south" of that sprawling river delta and the low damp-sheet hills beyond, all rearranged now by the geological upheaval of my movements. I sit there smoking and shivering and watching the dirty rainwater dripping onto the white tiles covering the floor of the room. The phonograph is playing "I May Never Go Home Anymore," and I know all the words, though I cannot remember ever having heard the song before.

"I have always loved her voice," the albino woman says from her place at the window, behind me and to my left.

"It's Marlene Dietrich, isn't it?" I ask, wishing I could say if I have always been afflicted with this patchwork memory. Perhaps this is merely the *nature* of memory, and that's something else I've forgotten.

"That wasn't her birth name," the white woman replies. "But it wasn't a stage name, either. Her parents named her Marie Magdalene—"

"Just like Jesus' whore," I say, interrupting. She ignores me.

"I read somewhere that Dietrich changed it, when she was still a teenager in Schöneberg. 'Marlene' is a contraction of 'Marie' and 'Magdalene.' Did you know that? I always thought that was quite clever of her."

I shrug and take a long drag on my cigarette, then glance at the scrapbook lying open on the bed next to me. The black-and-white photographs are all numbered, beginning with .0001, though I'm not at all sure they were the last time I went through it. The voice of the long dead actress fills the room, making it seem somehow warmer.

Don't ever think about tomorrow.

For tomorrow may never come.

"You should have another good look at the book," the albino woman suggests.

"I don't know what you expect me to see there. I don't understand what it is you want me to *tell* you. I've never *seen* that man before. I don't *remember* ever having seen that man before."

"Of course you don't. But you need to realise, we're running out of time. *You're* running out of time, love."

Time is nothing as long as I'm living it up this way.

I may never go home anymore.

I turn my head and watch her watching whatever lies on the other side of the windowpane. I still have not had the nerve to look for myself. Some part of me does not want to know, and some part of me still suspects there may be no more to the world than this room. If I look out that window, I might see nothing at all, because nothing may be all there is to see. When I fashioned the flat, rectangular world of the bed, and then this white room which must be the vault of the heavens which surrounds it, perhaps I stopped at the room's four walls. Plaster painted the same white as the floor tiles and the ceiling and the light shining down from those bare fluorescent stars. Beyond that, there is no more, the edges of my universe, the practical boundaries of my cosmic bubble.

"She really did a number on your skull," the albino says. "I don't know how they expect me to get anything, between the goddamn firewall and what she did."

"What *did* she do?" I ask, not really wanting to know that either, but it doesn't matter, because the albino woman does not answer me. She's still naked, as am I. I still do not know her name. "Are we in Kyoto?" I ask.

"Why the hell would they bother slinging a wog sniper all the way the fuck to Japan?" she wants to know, and I have no answer for that. I seem to have no answers at all.

I've got kisses and kisses galore,

That have never been tasted before.

"Just be a good little girl and look at the book again," she says to me. "Maybe this time you'll see something that you've missed."

I breathe a grey cloud of smoke out through my nostrils, then pick the scrapbook up off the bed. The covers are very slightly damp from lying there on the damp sheets. I don't suppose it matters. I turn the pages and smoke my cigarette. The same careworn, hollow-eyed, middle-aged face looking back at me as before, staring back at whomever took all these pictures. I turn another page, coming to page number nine, the four photos designated .0033 through .0036, and none of it means any more to me than it did the last time.

"I think that I may remember a good deal about Kyoto," I say. "But I don't remember anything at all about Greece. And I don't *look* Greek, do I?"

"You don't look Japanese, either."

One last puff, then I drop the butt of my cigarette to the wet tiles, and it sizzles there for half a moment. I run my fingers slowly over the four glossy photographs on the page, as if touching them might make some sort of difference. And, as it happens, I do see a scar on the man's chin I hadn't noticed before. I examine some of the other pages, and the scar is there on every single one of them.

"If I don't find it, whatever it is you want me to find in here—"

"—there are going to be a lot of disappointed people, sunshine, and you'll be the first."

"Can I have another cigarette?" I ask her.

"Just look at the damned book," she replies, so that's what I do. It's open to page fifteen, .0057-.0060. I try focusing on what the man's wearing instead of his face, but all I can see is the collar of a light-coloured T-shirt, and it's the same in every photograph. My eyes are so tired, and I shut them for a moment. I can almost imagine that the flat illumination from the fluorescent bulbs is draining me somehow, diminishing me, both body and soul. But then I remember that the white woman took my soul when she fucked me, so never mind. I sit there with my eyes shut, listening to the dripping water and listening to Marlene Dietrich and wishing I could at least remember if I've ever had a name.

If you treat me right, this might be the night.
I may never go home, I may never go home.
I may never go home anymore.
I may never go home anymore.

08. The Fire Escape

When I found the umbrella leaning in one corner of the room and opened the window and climbed out onto the fire escape, she didn't try to stop me. She did not even say a word. And there is a world beyond the white room, after all. But it isn't Kyoto. It is no city that I have seen or even dreamt of before. It must *be* a city, because I cannot imagine what else it might possibly be. I'm sitting with the window and the redbrick wall of the motel on my right, my naked ass against the icy steel grating, and the falling rain is very loud on the clear polyvinyl canopy of the umbrella. I think I might never have been this cold in all my life, and I don't know why I didn't take her robe, as well. If I have clothes of my own, they are not anywhere to be found in the room.

I peer through the rain-streaked umbrella and try to find words that would do justice to the intricate, towering structures rising up all around me and the motel (that it is a motel, I will readily admit, is only a working assumption). But I know I don't possess that sort of vocabulary. Maybe the peculiar staccato language the albino woman spoke when she came, maybe it contains nouns and verbs equal to these things I see.

They are both magnificent and terrible, these edifices that might be buildings and railways, smokestacks and turbines, streets and chimneys and great glass atriums. They are awful. That word might come the closest, in all its connotations. I will not say they are beautiful, for there is something *loathsome* about these bizarre structures. At least, to me they seem bizarre; I cannot say with any certainty that they are. Possibly, I am the alien here, me and this unremarkable redbrick motel. Thinking through this amnesiac mist locked up inside my head, there is no solid point of reference left to me, no objective standard by which I may judge. There is only gut reaction, and my gut reaction is that they are bizarre and loathsome things.

The air out here smells like rain and ozone, carbon monoxide and chemicals I do not know the names for, and yet it still smells very much cleaner than the white room with its soggy miasma of mold and slow decay.

These spiraling, jointed, ribsy things which *might* be the skyscrapers of an unnamed or unnamable city, they are as intricate as the calcareous or chitinous skeletons of deep-sea creatures. There. I *do* have a few words, though they are utterly insufficient. They are mere *approximations* of what I see. So, yes, they seem organic, as though they are the product not of conscious engineering and construction but of evolution and ontogeny. They have *grown* here, I think—all of them—and I wonder if the men and women who planted the necessary seeds or embryos, how ever many ages ago, are anything like the albino who took my soul away.

And then I hear the noise of vast machineries…no, I have been *hearing* this noise all along, but only now has my amazement or apprehension or awe at the sight of this city dimmed enough that I look for the source of the sounds. And I see, not far away, there is a sort of clearing in this urban, industrial carapace. And I can see the muddy earth ripped open there, red as a wound in any living creature. There are great indescribable contraptions busy making the wound much larger, gouging and drilling out buckets or mouthfuls of mud and meat to be dumped upon steaming spoilage heaps or fed onto conveyer belts that stretch away into the foggy distance.

And there is something in that hole, something still only partly exposed by the exertions of these machines that might not be machines at all. Something I know (and no, I cannot say how I could ever *know* such a thing) has lain there undisturbed and sleeping for millennia, and now they mean to wake it up.

I look away. I've seen too much already.

Something is creeping slowly along the exterior of one of the strange buildings, and it might be a living tumor—a malignant mass of tissue and corruption and ideas—and, then again, it might be nothing more than an elevator.

Then I hear knuckles rapping a windowpane, and when I turn my head back towards the motel, the albino woman is watching me with her bright blue eyes.

07. The Book (II)

Don't ever think about tomorrow.
For tomorrow may never come.

And then the albino woman lifts the phonograph needle from the record and, instantly, the music goes away. I wish she had let it keep on playing, over and over and over, because now the unceasing *drip drip drip* from the ceiling to the tiles seems so much louder than when I had the song and Marlene Dietrich's voice to concentrate on. The woman turns on her whirring robotic legs and stares at me.

"You never did tell me what happened to your arm," she says and smiles.

"Did you ask?"

"I believe that I did, yes."

I am sitting there at the foot of the bed with the scrapbook lying open on my lap, my shriveled left arm held close to my chest. And it occurs to me that I do not *know* what happened to my arm, and also it occurs to me that I have no recollection whatsoever of there being anything at all wrong with it before she asked how it got this way. And then this *third* observation, which seems only slightly less disconcerting than having forgotten that I'm a cripple (like her), and that I must have been a cripple for a very long time: the book is open to photos .0705-.0708, page 177, and I notice that beside each photo's number are distinct and upraised dimples, like Braille, though I do not know for certain this *is* Braille. I flip back a few pages and see that, yes, the dimples are there on every page.

"That's very thoughtful," I say, so softly that I am almost whispering. "I might have been blind, after all."

"You might be yet," the white woman says.

"If I were," I reply without looking up from the book, "I couldn't even see the damned photographs, much less find whatever it is you *think* I can find in here."

"You don't get off that easily," she laughs, and her noisy mechanical legs carry her from the table with the phonograph to the bed, and she begins the arduous and apparently painful process of detaching herself from the contraptions. I try to focus on the book, trying not to watch the albino or hear the dripping ceiling or smell the dank stench of the room. Trying only to see the photographs. I don't ask why anyone would bother to provide Braille numbers for photographs that a blind person could not see. And this time, she kindly does not answer my unasked question. I return to page 177, then proceed to 178, then on to 179.

"Shit," the albino woman hisses, forcing her curse out through clenched teeth as she disconnects the primary neural lead to her right thigh. There's thick, dark pus and a bead of fresh blood clinging to the plug. More pus leaks from the port and runs down the stump of her leg.

"Is it actually worth all that trouble and discomfort?" I ask. "Wouldn't a wheelchair be—"

"Why don't you try to mind your own goddamn business," she barks at me, and so I do. I go back to the scrapbook, back to photos .0713-.0716 and that face I know I will be seeing for a long time to come, whenever I shut my eyes. I will see him in my sleep, if I am allowed to live long enough to ever sleep again.

The woman sighs a halting, painful sort of sigh and eases herself back onto the sheets, freed now from the prosthetics, which are left standing side by side at the foot of the bed.

"I picked up a patch bug a while back," she says. "Some sort of cross-scripting germ, a quaint little XSSV symbiote. But it's being treated. It's nothing lethal."

And that's when I see it. She's stretched out there next to me talking about viruses and slow-purge reboots, and I notice the puffy reddish rim surrounding photograph number .0715. This *page* is infected, like the albino woman and her robotic legs, and the *site* of the infection is right here beneath .0715.

"I think I've found it," I say and press the pad of my thumb gently to the photograph. It's hot to the touch, and I can feel something moving about beneath the haggard face of the man with the shaved head and the scar on his chin.

She props herself up on her elbows when I hold the scrapbook out so that she can see. "Well, well," she says. "Maybe you have, and maybe you haven't. Either way, sunshine, it's going to hurt when you pull that scab away."

"Is that what I'm supposed to do?" I ask her, laying the heavy scrapbook back across my lap. Even as I watch, the necrosis has begun to spread across the page towards the other three photographs.

"Do it quickly," she says, and I can hear the eagerness in her voice. "Like pulling off a sticky plaster. Do it fast, and maybe it'll hurt less."

"Is *this* what you wanted me to find? Is this it?"

"You're stalling," she says. "Just fucking do it."

And then the black telephone begins to ring again.

09. Exit Music (The Gun)

Sitting beneath the transparent canopy of the borrowed umbrella, sitting naked in the rain on the fire escape, and now she's standing over me, held up by all those shiny chrome struts and gears and pistons. She did not even have to open the window or climb out over the sill, but I can not ever explain, in words, how it was she exited the room. It only matters that she did. It only matters that she's standing over me holding the Beretta 9mm, aiming it at my head.

"I never made any promises," she tells me, and I nod (because that's true) and lower the umbrella and fold it shut. I support my useless left arm with my right and stare directly up into the cold rain, wishing there were anything falling from that leaden sky clean enough to wash away the weight of all these things I cannot remember or will never be permitted to remember.

"The war isn't going well," she says. "We've lost Hsinchu and Changhua. I think we all know that Taipei can't be far behind. Too many feedback loops. Way too many scratch hits."

"Nothing to be desired anymore," I say, and taste the bitter, toxic raindrops on my tongue.

"Nothing at all," she tells me, setting the muzzle of the M9 to my right temple. I am already so chilled I do not feel the cold steel, only the pressure of the gun against my skin. The rain stings my eyes, and I blink. I take a deep breath and try not to shiver.

"Whatever they're digging up over there," and I nod towards the excavations, "they should stop. You should tell them that soon, before they wake it up."

"You think they'd listen...to someone like me?" she asks. "Is that what you think?"

"I don't know what I think anymore."

Above me and all around me this lifeless, living husk that might be a city or only the mummified innards of some immense biomechanoid crustacean goes on about its clockwork day-to-day affairs, all its secret metabolisms, its ancient habits. It does not see me—or seeing me, it shows even less regard for me than I might show a single mite nestled deep within a single eyelash follicle. I gaze up at that inscrutable tangle of spires and flying buttresses, rotundas and acroterion flourishes and all the thousands of solemn gushing rainspouts.

"Do not feel unloved," she says, and I shut my eyes and sense all the world move beneath me.

Ode to Katan Amano

No one hears when I ease the heavy steel door shut behind me. All the ears in the darkened workshop, all those hundreds and hundreds of ears, but still no one hears a thing. And I stand there for a while, as unmoving as they, not exactly frightened and not exactly uncertain if I should see this through—I think I stand there in reverence. I believe that's the word that people use for what I feel in that moment, standing there alone, alone with that assembled crowd. I can hear a clock ticking somewhere in the room, counting off small bits of eternity. I can hear cars and trucks down on the street below. I can hear people on the sidewalk outside the building. But there is a silence, nonetheless. I imagine it is an *expectant* silence, that they are all waiting to see what I'll do next. And I realize that I'm waiting to learn the very same thing.

What will I do next?

I remember the small flashlight clipped to my key chain, and I thumb its on/off switch, then shine the narrow white beam about the cavernous room. Their painted faces stare back at me. It's almost disconcerting, almost uncanny, and it occurs to me that, to some others, there would no doubt be a sort of horror at finding themselves standing in the dark among these countless dolls, puppets, the marionettes, mannequins, maquettes, life casts, death masks...all these facsimiles of humanity, grotesque and beautiful and absurd likenesses shaped from clay and plasticine, wood and *papier-mâché*. I take a deep breath. The room smells like work, like creation—wood shavings, latex, acrylics and oils, sawdust, linseed and turpentine, acetone, alginate and silicone compounds, dust and oil. I never imagined there would be so many competing smells, perhaps because the object of my concern has seemed always so visual and tactile that I've neglected that sense. But now I understand that these odors are an essential aspect of this place. They are the birthing smells, and the dying smells, too, and I *should* have anticipated them.

I take three steps, coming to a long table or work bench. There are jars with glass eyes mounted on metal rods—green, brown, hazel, crimson—and tools, most of which I recognize but don't know the names for. There's part of a human skeleton, a shoulder and left arm dangling on a metal armature. There's a cat's skeleton, too. There are clamps and spools of wire, a cardboard box filled with springs, calipers and tubes of glue. And I know that I'm being distracted, that none of this is what I've come here to see, what I've *broken in* to see, and I remind myself that I may be discovered at any moment, especially with the flashlight, and I should make better use of the time I have. It's not the mere *craft* that's brought me here, and I check my watch. Twelve minutes past two in the morning. I have half an hour before security checks this floor again, if the schedules can be trusted. I suspect that trespassers, trespassers who would be mistaken for thieves, cannot trust schedules or much of anything else.

"You won't reconsider this?" you asked me, just a couple of hours ago, and I almost didn't answer. I almost left without bothering to say that I would not.

"I wish you would come with me," I said.

"That's stupid," you said. "Two would be even more likely to be caught than would one."

"With two, one can be a look-out," I suggested.

"You know how you sound? You sound like a child playing cops and robbers. Besides, why would I want to waste my evening being your look-out."

"We could take turns."

You lit a cigarette and switched on the television. "I'm not going to talk about this anymore. Do what you want. But don't call me to bail you out."

I step past the table, past a rack supporting an assortment of Japanese-style Bunraku puppets—moon-faced geishas, two gold- and red-robed Samurai, a fanged demon with green skin and black eyes like pools of loss. There's another table, this one crowded by the legs, arms, and torsos of several dismantled department-store mannequins. None have heads, and there is not a head anywhere on the table.

"It's ghoulish," you said, but that was *last* night. "It's an unhealthy preoccupation. It's something that we ought to speak with Dr. Bolen about."

I said something about irony, something that made you angry, but then we fucked anyway.

And here *she* is, the one I have come for, here on a pedestal, surrounded by a motley entourage of angels and Greek heroines, an old man seated before a miniature typewriter, a beautiful bronze woman with the horns of an antelope. But the bronze woman is not half so beautiful as the one the sculptor has named Sanctuary. I whisper her name aloud, *Sanctuary*. There is a flutter in my belly, and another flutter between my legs, and I want to sit down, want to kneel, but I only stand there, staring at her.

"I could stop you from going," you said to me, last night. "It's within my rights. I could stop you."

"Yes," I replied. "You could. You could do that."

"I should," you said, taking off your clothes, undressing in front of the mirror and watching my reflection.

"Is that what I am to you?" I asked.

"Fuck you. That was a shitty thing to say."

"Was it? I'm not so sure."

I first saw "Sanctuary" during an exhibition of dolls and puppetry at MoMA, and then I bought a book with two photographs of her inside. When you threw the book out, I bought another copy and hid it where I knew you'd never think to look. And now

I am standing here in front of her again, and this time there is no museum-glass barrier between us. I could touch her now. I could raise my hand and place it gently against her Dresden-blue forehead. She watches me, neither encouraging nor discouraging, merely waiting for whatever it is that I'll decide. Sanctuary's own arms are held close to her body, her exquisite hands with their nails the color of altar candles. Her left hand is clenched into something just short of a fist.

"It's the truth," you said, sitting down on the bed, and you looked at me over your shoulder. "It's not something I enjoy pointing out, but it's the truth, anyway."

"I'm your property," I said and began unbuttoning my blouse. "I'm only a slave."

"I never said that. You know damn well that I've never thought of you that way."

The sculptor has dressed her in delicate folds of silk damask, a silver sash, a gathered long skirt of some metallic fabric decorated with the iridescent shells of tiny snails; garments borrowed from some imaginary nationality. There are definite hints of Asian and African influences, but the ultimate effect is something novel, something that would never have existed had the artist not willed it into being. I shine the flashlight across her face, and the light picks out the finest details, her minute eyelashes, creases at the corners of her mouth, a purple scar on her blue cheek.

"You treat it like some fucking idol," you said, once I'd undressed and stood naked in front of you. "Is that what she's become? Your Virgin Mary, a goddamn plaster saint for you to fawn over and pray to? Is she going to answer your prayers?"

"She's only a doll," I said, as you roughly peeled back the flaps of artificial flesh concealing my ventral data ports. You plugged in the first cable, just above my navel. You've always loved that joke, that I *have* a navel. "The artifice of history," you said once. There was a dull whir and a click as the cable screwed itself firmly into place, a centimeter beneath my skin, and I closed my eyes, as if that would keep me from seeing the images waiting for me only a little farther along.

Sanctuary's face is turned upwards very slightly, her grey eyes fixed on some point behind and far above my head. I don't turn to see, perhaps because I'm afraid that I *would* see.

When all the black cables were in place, the last one plugged into the socket between my breasts, and you'd jacked me into the big subprocessor stashed beneath our bed, you lay back in the sheets and told me to take off my face. You'd only ever done that once before, the same night that you threw the first book out, so I understood *why* you were doing it.

"Does humiliating me make me more yours?" I asked. "Is that the way it seems to you?"

"Something like that," you said and smiled. "Come on. Hurry it up. Don't take all goddamn night about it. Show me what's *under* there."

"I would ask permission," I tell Sanctuary, and I would, if I thought she could answer me. Touching her without some encouragement or consent feels like a violation. But I *do* touch her. That's why I've come here. That's why I paid an intern more than two hundred dollars for the access codes to the first floor and the elevator. My fingertips brush the hem of her skirt, hesitating a moment before they slip underneath the fabric. Her expression does not change; her eyes are still staring towards Heaven.

"I don't want to," I told you.

"I *know* that. But you *will* do it."

There's a sort of petticoat beneath her skirt, soft cotton like a second line of defence, and I pause. I might have heard a sound out in the hallway, but I'm not sure. I listen for a minute, two, three, but the sound isn't repeated. *No one's out there*, I tell myself. *Don't be afraid. You won't get a second chance.*

My fingers wander into the darkness past the petticoat, and I find her legs. I find that she *has* legs; it was always a possibility that she wouldn't. But there they are, not unlike my navel, something superfluous that the artist felt compelled to include, something

Sanctuary would not have been complete without. She's even wearing stockings; they feel like nylon.

"Take it off," you said again, and I pressed the release tab beneath my chin, and there was a faint hydraulic whine before it popped free. I handed it to you, because I knew that's what you wanted. You laughed and held it up in front of your own face like a carnival masquerade, your eyes peering back at me through the holes made for my eyes.

"What do you think?" you asked, and laughed again.

"I think you're a bitch," I replied, and that only made you laugh louder.

You laid my face aside then and strapped on the dildo you brought home from Amsterdam last year, the one built by the same company that made me. And you fucked me while the cables streamed images of murder and war and slow death, slaughter-house floors slick with blood and a young man masturbating while he writhes inside a scatter of rusted metal and broken glass. I did not watch, but I did see it all, superimposed over you.

"And they can survive treatment that would kill live actors. When I first saw them in my boyhood nothing delighted me more than when all the puppets went up in a balloon and presently dropped from the skies with an appalling crash on the floor." I found that in a book by George Bernard Shaw. *They can survive treatment that would kill live actors.*

"Tell me to stop," I say, but Sanctuary doesn't reply, and she does not look at me. My fingers move past her perfect calves, past her knees, finding her thighs. "Please, tell me to stop," I say again, almost begging now, as if I believe that she can answer me.

"Hell, go if that's what you want," you told me just before I left our apartment to take the subway down to Chinatown. "If it'll get this out of your system, do it. I'm sick to fucking death of hearing about the goddamn doll. And if they catch you, no one's gonna ask twice if I request a memory wipe. Maybe you ought to think about that."

And I did. I thought about that all the way to the old building with the sculptor's studio.

"It's okay," I tell Sanctuary. "I can hear you anyway. You don't have to speak for me to hear." And I slip my hand out from beneath her skirt. She doesn't look relieved or grateful or frightened that I might change my mind. She only looks the way that the sculptor has built her to look. I stand there for another ten or fifteen minutes, listening to the ticking clock and the traffic down on the street, alone in the company of Sanctuary and the bronze woman, the man with the typewriter and the angel with its broad eggshell wings. And then I touch Sanctuary's blue face one last time, one last time to sustain me forever, and leave the workshop as silently as I came in.

"The puppet was meant to turn into a monster. But an unsummoned monster can appear, unless the artist is careful."

Elizabeth King (1999)

A Season of Broken Dolls

August 14, 2027

Sabit's the one with a hard-on for stitchwork, not me. It is not exactly (or at all) my particular realm of expertise, not my cuppa, not my *scene*—as the beatniks used to say, back there in those happy Neolithic times. I mean the plethora of Lower Manhattan flesh-art dives like Guro/Guro or Twist or that pretentious little shitstain way down on Pearl—*Corpus Ex Machina*—the one that gets almost as much space in the police blotters as in the glossy snip-art rags. Me, I'm still laboring alone or nearly so in the Dark Ages, and she never lets me forget it. My unfashionable and unprofitable preoccupation with mere canvas and paint, steel and plaster, all that which has been deemed *démodé, passé,* Post-Relevant, all that which is fit only to fill up musty old museum vaults and public galleries, gathering more dust even than my career. *You still write on a goddamn keyboard, for chris'sakes,* she laughs. *You're the only woman I ever fucked made being a living fossil a goddamn point of pride.* And then Sabit checks for my pulse—two fingers pressed gently to a wrist or the side of my throat—bcause, hey, maybe I'm not a *living* fossil at all. Maybe I'm that *other* kind, like Pollack and Mondrian, Henry Moore and poor old Man Ray. *No, no, no, the blood's still flowing sluggishly along,* she smiles and lights a cigarette. *Too bad. Maybe there's hope for you yet, my love.* Sabit likes to talk almost as much as she likes to watch. It's not as though the bitch has a mark on her hide anywhere, not as though she's anything but a tourist with a hard-on, a fetishist who can not ever get enough of her kink. Prick her for a crimson bead and the results would come back same as mine, 98% the same as any chimpanzee. She knows how much contempt is reserved in those quarters for tourists and trippers, but I think that only makes her more zealous. She exhales, and smoke lingers like a unearned halo about her face. I should have dumped her months ago, but I'm not as young as I used to be, and I'm just as addicted to sex as she is to nicotine and pills and stitchwork. She calls herself a poet, but she has never let me read a word she's written, if she's ever written a word. I found her a year ago, almost a year ago, found her in a run-down titty bar getting fucked-up on vodka and laudanum and speed and the too-firm silicone breasts of women who might have been the real thing—even if their perfect boobs were not—or might only have been cheap japandroids. She followed me home, fifteen years my junior, and the more things change, the more things stay the way they were day before day before yesterday, day before I met Sabit and her slumberous Arabian eyes. My sloe-eyed stitch-fiend of a girlfriend, and I have her, and she has me, and we're as happy as happy can be, and I pretend it means something more than orgasms and not being alone, something more than me annoying her and her taunting ~~and insulting~~ me. Now she's telling me there's a new line-up down @ *Corpus Ex Machina* (hereafter known simply as *CeM*), and we have to be there tomorrow night. *We have to be there,* she says. *The Trenton Group is showing, and last time the Trenton Group showed, there was almost a riot, so we have to be there.* I have deadlines that have nothing whatsoever to do with that constantly revolving meat-market spectacle, and in a moment I'll finish this entry & then I'll tell her that, and she'll tell me we have to be there, we have to be there, & there will be time to finish my articles later. There always is, & I'm never late. Never late enough to matter. I'll go with her, bcause I do not trust her to go alone—not go alone *and* come back here again— she'll tell me that, and she'll be right as fucking rain. Her smug triumph, well that's a given. Just as my obligatory refusal followed by inevitable, reluctant acquiescence is also a given. We play by the same rules every time. Now she's on about some scandal @ Guro/ Guro—chicanery and artifice, prosthetics, and she says, *They're all a bunch of gidding poseurs, the shitheels run that sorry dump. Someone ought to burn it to the ground for this.* You know how to light a match I reply, & she rolls her dark eyes @ me. No rain today. No rain since…June. The sky at noon is the color of rust, and I wish it were winter. Enough for now. Maybe she'll shut up for 10 or 15 if I fuck her.

August 16, 2027

"You're into that whole *scene*, right?" Which only shows to go once again that my editor still has her head rammed so far up her ass that her farts smell like toothpaste. But I said yeah, sure, bcause she wanted someone with cred on the Guro/Guro story, the stitch chicanery, allegations of fraud among the freaks, & what else was I supposed to say? I can't remember the last time I had the nerve to turn down a paying assignment. Must have been years before I met Sabit, at least. So, yeah, I tagged along last night, just like she wanted—both of them wanted—she & she, but @ least I can say it's work, and Berlin picked up the tab. Sabit's out, so I don't have her yammering in my goddamn ear, an hour to myself, perhaps, half an hour, however long it takes her to get back with dinner. I wanted to put something down, something that isn't in the notes and photos I've already filed with the pre-edit gleets. Fuck. I've been popping caps from Sabit's pharmacopoeia all goddamn day long, I don't even know what, the baby-blue ones she gets $300/ two dozen from Peru, the ones she says calm her down but they're not calming me down. They haven't even dulled the edge, so far as I can tell. But, anyway, there we were @ CeM, in the crowded Pearl St. warehouse passing itself off as a slaughterhouse or a zoo or an exhibition or what the fuck ever, and there's this bird from Tokyo, and I never got her name, but she had eyes all the colors of peacock feathers, iridescent eyes, and she recognized me. Some monied bird with pretty peacock eyes. She'd read the series I wrote in '21 when the city finally gave up and let the sea have the subway. *I read a lot,* she said. *I might have been a journalist myself,* she said. That sort of shit. Thought she was going to ask me to sign a goddamn cocktail napkin. And I'm smiling & nodding yes, bcause that's agency policy, be nice to the readers, don't feed the pigeons, whatever. But I can't take my eyes off the walls. The walls are new. They were just walls last time Sabit dragged me down to one of her snip affairs. Now they're alive, every square inch, mottled shades of pink and gray and whatever you call that shade between pink and gray. Touch them (Sabit must have touched them a hundred times) and they twitch or sprout goose bumps. They sweat, those walls. And the peacock girl was in one ear, and Sabit was in the other, the music so loud I was already getting a headache before my fourth drink, and I was trying to stop looking at those walls. *Pig,* Sabit told me later in the evening. *It's all just pig,* and she sounded disappointed. Most of this is in the notes, though I didn't say how unsettling I found those walls of skin. I save the revulsion for my own dime. Sabit says they're working on adding functional genitalia and...fuck. I hear her at the door. Later, then. She has to shut up and go to sleep eventually.

August 16, 2027 (later, 11:47 p.m.)

Sabit came back with a bag full of Indian takeaway, when she'd gone out for sushi. I really couldn't care less, one way or the other, these days food is only fucking food—curry or wasabi, but when I *asked* why she'd changed her mind, she just stared at me, eyes blank as a goddamn dead codfish, & shrugged. Then she was quiet all night long, & the last thing I need just now is Sabit Abbasi going all silent and creepy on me. She's asleep, snoring bcause her sinuses are bad bcause she smokes too much. & I'm losing the momentum I needed to say *anything* more about what happened @ CeM on Sat. night. It's all fading, like a dream.

I've been reading one of Sabit's books, *The Breathing Composition* (Welleran Smith, 2025), something from those long-ago days when the *avant-garde* abomination of stitch & snip was still hardly more than nervous rumor & theory & the wishful thinking of a handful of East Coast art pervs. I don't know what I was looking for, if it was just research for the article, don't know what I thought I might find—or what any of this has to do with Sat. nite. Am I afraid to write it down? That's what Sabit would say. But I won't ask Sabit. What do *you* dream, Sabit, my dear sadistic plaything? Do you *dream* in installations, muscles and tendons, gallery walls of sweating pig flesh, living bone exposed for all to see, vivisection as not-quite still life, portrait of the artist as a young atrocity? Are your sweet dreams the same things keeping me awake, making me afraid to sleep? There was so goddamn much @ CeM to turn my fucking stomach, but just this one thing has me jigged and sleepless and popping your blue Peruvian bon bons. Just this one thing. I'm not the squeamish sort, and everyone knows it. That's one reason the agency tossed the Guro/Guro story at me. Gore & sex and mutilation? Give it to Schuler. She's seen the worst and keeps coming back for more. Wasn't she one of the first into Brooklyn after the bomb? & she did that crazy whick out on the Stuyvesant rat attacks. How many murders and suicides and serial killers does that make for Schuler now? 9? Fourteen? 38? That kid in the Bronx, the Puerto Rican bastard who sliced up his little sister & then fed her through a food processor, that was one of Schuler's, yeah? *Ad infinitum, ad nauseam*, hail Mary, full of beans. Cause they know I won't be on my knees puking up lunch when I should be making notes & getting the vid or asking questions. But now, *now* Sabit, I'm dancing round this one thing. This one little thing. So, here there's a big ol' chink in these renowned nerves of steel. Maybe I've got a weak spot after fucking all. Rings of flesh, towers of iron—oh yeah, sure—fucking corpses heaped in dumpsters and rats eating fucking babies alive & winos & don't forget the kid with the Cuisinart—sure, fine—but that one labeled #17, oh, now *that's* another goddamn story. She *saw* something there, & ol' Brass-Balls Schuler was never quite the same again, isn't that the way it goes?

Are you laughing in your dreams, Sabit? Is that why you're smiling next to me in your goddamn sleep? I've dog-eared a page in your book, Sabit, a page with a poem written in a New Jersey loony bin by a woman, & Welleran Smith just calls her Jane Doe so I do not know her name. But Welleran Smith & that mangy bunch of stitch prophets called her a visionary, & I'm writing it down here, while I try to find the nerve to say whatever it is I'd wanted to say about #17:

> *spines and bellies knitted & proud and all open*
> *all watching spines and bellies and the three;*
> *triptych & buckled, ragdoll fusion*
> *3 of you so conjoined, my eyes from yours,*
> *arterial hallways knitted red proud flesh*
> *Healing and straining for cartilage & epidermis*
> *Not taking, we cannot imagine*
> *So many wet lips, your sky Raggedy alchemy*
> *And all expecting Jerusalem*

And Welleran Smith, he proclaims Jane Doe a "hyperlucid transcendent schizo-oracle," a "visionary calling into the maelstrom." & turns out, here in the footnotes, they put the bitch away bcause she'd drugged her lover—she was a lesbian; of course, she had to be a lesbian—she drugged her lover and used surgical thread to sew the woman's lips & nostrils closed, *after* performing a crude tracheotomy so she wouldn't suffocate. Jane Doe sewed her own vagina shut, and she removed her own nipples & then tried grafting them onto her gf's belly. She kept the woman (not named, sorry, lost to anonymity) cuffed to a bed for almost 6 weeks before someone finally came poking around & jesus fucking christ, Sabit, this is the sort of sick bullshit set it all in motion. Jane Doe's still locked away in her padded cell, I'm guessing—*hyperlucid* & worshipped by the snips—& maybe the woman she mutilated is alive somewhere, trying to forget. Maybe the doctors even patched her up (ha ha fucking ha). Maybe even made her good as new again, but I doubt it. I need to sleep. I need to lie down & close my eyes & not see #17 and sweating walls and Sabit ready to fucking cum bcause she can never, ever get enough. It's half an hour after midnight, & they expect copy from me tomorrow night, eight sharp, when I haven't written a goddamn word about the phony stitchwork @ Guro/Guro. Fuck you, Sabit, and fuck Jane Doe & that jackoff Welleran Smith and the girl with peacock eyes that I should have screwed just to piss you off. I should have brought her back here and fucked her in our bed, & maybe you'd have found some other snip tourist & even now I could be basking in the sanguine cherry glow of happily ever fucking after.

August 18, 2027

I'm off the Guro/Guro story. Missed the *extended* DL tonight, no copy, never even made it down to the gallery. Just my notes and photos from CeM for someone else to pick up where I left off. Lucky the agency didn't let me go. Lucky or unlucky. But they can't can me, not for missing a deadline or two. I have rep, I have creds, I have awards & experience & loyal goddamn readers. Hell, I still get a byline on this thing; it's in my contract. Fuck it. Fuck it all.

August 19, 2027

Welleran Smith's "Jane Doe" died about six months ago, back in March. I asked some questions, said it was work for the magazine, tagged some people who know people who could get to the files. It was a suicide—oh, and never you mind that she'd been on suicide watch for years. This one was a certified trooper, a bona-fide martyr in the service of her own undoing. She chewed her tongue in half & choked herself on it. She had a name, too. Don't know if Smith knew it & simply withheld it, or if he never looked that far. Maybe he only prigged the bits he needed to put the snips in orbit & disregarded the rest. "Jane Doe" was Judith Louise Darger, born 1992, Ph. D. in Anthropology from Yale, specialized in urban neomythology, syncretism, etc. & did a book with HarperC back in '21—*Bloody Mary, La Llorona, and the Blue Lady: Feminine Icons in a Fabricated Child's Apocalypse*. Sold for shit, out of print by 2023. But found a battered copy cheap uptown. Darger's gf and victim, she's dead, too. Another suicide, not long after they put Darger away. Turns out, she had a history of neurosis and self-mutilation going back to high school, & there was all sorts of shit there I'm not going to get into, but she told the courts that what Darger did to her, and to herself, they'd planned the whole thing for months. So, why the fuck did good old Welleran Smith leave *that* part out? It was in the goddamn press, no secret. I have a photograph of Judith Darger, right here on the dj of her book. She could not look less remarkable. Sabit says there's another Trenton Group show this weekend & don't I wanna to go? She's hardly said three words to me the last couple of days, but she told me this. Get another look at #17, she said, & I almost fucking hit her. No more pills, Schuler. No more pills.

August 20, 2027

No sleep last night. Today, I filed for my next assignment, but so far the green bin's still empty. Maybe I'm being punished for blowing the DL on Weds. night, some sort of pass-ag bullshit bcause that's the best those weasels in senior edit can ever seem to manage. Or maybe it's only a sloooowwwww week. I am having a hard time caring, either way. No sleep last night. No, I said that already. Time on my hands and that's never a good thing.

Insomnia and coffee and gin, takeaway and Pop-Tarts and a faint throb that wants to be a headache (how long since one of those?), me locked in my office last night reading a few chapters of Darger's grand flop, but there's nothing in there—fascinating and I don't know why it wasn't better received, but still leading me nowhere, nowhere at all (where did I *think* it would lead?). This bit re: La Llorona ("Bloody Mary") from Ch. 3—"Some girls with no home feel claws scratching under the skin on their arms. Their hand [sic] looks like red fire." And this one, from a *Miami New Times* article: "When a child says he got the story from the spirit world, as homeless children do, you've hit the ultimate *non sequitur*." Homeless kids and demons and angels, street gangs, drugs, the socioeconomic calamities of thirty goddamn years ago. News articles from 1997. A journalistic scam. None of this is gonna answer any of my questions, if I truly have questions to be answered. But this is "Jane Doe's" magnum opus, and there is some grim fascination I can't shake—How did she get from *there* to *there*, from phony diy street myths to sewing her gf's mouth shut? Maybe it wasn't such a short goddamn walk. Maybe, one night, she stood before a dark mirror in a darkened room, the mirror coated with dried saltwater—going native or just too fucking curious, whatever—and maybe she *stood* there chanting *Bloody Mary, Bloody Mary*, over and over and over and La Llorona scratched her way out through the looking glass, scarring the anthropologist's soul with her rosary beads. Maybe that's where this began, the snips and stitches, #17. Maybe it all goes back to those homeless kids in Miami, back before the flood, before the W. Antarctic ice sheet melted and Dade County FL sank like a stone, and all along it was the late Dr. J. L. Darger let this djinn out of its bottle in ways people like Sabit have not yet begun to suspect and never will. I'm babbling, and if that's the best I can do, I'm going to stop keeping a damned journal. I've agreed to be @ CeM tomorrow night with Sabit. I'm a big girl. I can sip my shitty Merlot and nibble greasy orange cheese and stale crackers with the best of them. I can bear the soulless conversation and the sweating porcine walls. I can look at #17 and see nothing there but bad art, fucked-up artless crap, pretentious carnage and willful suffering. Maybe then I can put *all* this shit behind me. Who knows, maybe I can even put Sabit behind me, too.

August 20, 2027 (later, p.m.)

Sabit says the surgeon on #17 will be at the show t'morrow night. I think maybe it's someone Sabit was screwing before she started screwing me. Oh, & this, from *The Breathing Composition*, which I've started reading again & frankly wish I had not. Seems Welleran Smith somehow got his paws on Darger's diary, or *one* of her diaries, & he quotes it at length (& no doubt there are contextual issues; don't know the fate of the original text):

"We are all alone on a darkling plain, precisely as Matt. Arnold said. We are so very alone here, and we yearn each day for the reunification promised by priests and gurus and by some ancient animal instinct. We are evolution's grand degenerates, locked away forever in the consummate prison cells of our conscious minds, each divided always from the other. I met a man from Spain, and he gave me a note card with the number seventeen written on it seventeen times. He thought that surely I would understand right away, and he was heartbroken when I did not. When I asked, he would not explain. I've kept the card in my files, and sometimes I take it out and stare at it, hoping that I will at last discern its message. But it remains perfectly opaque, bcause my eyes are the eyes of the damned."

& I'm looking thru the program for the Trenton Show on the 15th, last Sun., & only one piece is *numbered*, only 1 piece w/a # for a title—#17. Yes, I know. I'm going in circles here. Chasing my own ass. Toys in the attic. Nutters as the goddamn snips if I don't watch myself. If I don't get some sleep. I haven't seen Sabit all evening, just a call this afternoon.

August 21, 2027 (Saturday, 10:12 a.m.)

Four whole hours sleep last night. & the hangover is not so bad that old-fash blck coffee and aspirin isn't helping. My head feels clearer than it has in days. Sabit came home sometime after I nodded off & I woke with her snoring next to me. When I asked if maybe she wanted breakfast, she smiled, so I made eggs & cut a grapefruit in half. Perhaps I can persuade her to stay home tonight, that we should *both* stay home tonight. There is nothing down there I need to see again.

August 21, 2027 (2:18 p.m.)

No, she says. *We are expected,* she says, & what the fuck is that supposed to mean, anyway? So there was a fight, bcause there always has to be a fight with Sabit, a real screamer this time, & I have no idea where she's run off to but she swore she'd be back by *five* & I better be sober, she said, & I better be dressed & ready for the show. So, yeah, fuck it. I'll go to the damn show with her. I'll rub shoulders with the stitch freaks this one last time. Maybe I'll even have a good long look at #17 (tho' now, I should add, now Sabit says the surgeon won't be there after all). Maybe I'll stand & stare until it's only flesh & wires & hooks & fancy lighting. Sidonie-Gabrielle Colette wrote somewhere, "Look for a long time at what pleases you, and for a longer time at what pains you." Maybe I'll shame them all with my staring. They only feel as much pain as they *want* to feel—isn't that what Sabit is always telling me? The stitchworks, they get all the best painkillers, ever since the Feds decided this sick shit constitutes Art—so long as certain lines are not crossed. They bask in glassy-eyed morphine hazes, shocked cold orange on neuroblocks & Fibrodene & Elyzzium, exotic transdermals & maybe all that shit's legal & maybe it ain't, but 2380 no one's asking too many questions as the City of NY has enough on its great collective plate these days w/out stitch-friendly lawyers raising a holy funk about censorship and freedom of expression and 1st Amendment violations. The cops hate the fuckers, but none of the arrests have had jack to do with drugs, just disorderly conduct, riots after shows, shit like that. But yeah, t'morrow night I'll go back to CeM with Sabit, my heart's damned desire, my cunt's lazy love, & I will look until they want to fucking charge me extra.

August 21, 2027

So Sabit shows up an hour or so after dark...she's gone now, gone again bcause I suppose I have chased her away, again. That's what she would say, I am sure. I have chased her away again. But, as I was saying, she shows up, & I can tell she's been drinking bcause she has that smirk and that swagger she gets when she's been drinking, & I can tell she's still pissed. I'm waiting for the other shoe. I'm waiting, bcause I fucking know whatever's coming next is for my benefit. & I'm thinking, screw it, get it over with, don't let her have the satisfaction of getting in the first blow. I'm thinking, this is where it ends. Tonight. No more of her bullshit. It's been a grandiose act of reciprocal masochism, Sabit, & it's been raw & all, but enough's enough. @ least the sex was good, so let's remember that & move on. & that's when I notice the gauze patch taped to her back, centered between her shoulder blades just so, placed *just so* there between her scapulae, centered on the smooth brown plain of her trapezius (let me write this the way a goddamn snip would write it, cluttered with an anatomist's Latin). & when I ask her what the fuck, she just shrugs, & that swatch of gauze goes up & then down again. But I know. I know whatever it is she's done, whatever comes next, this is it. This is her preemptive volley, so I can just forget all about landing the first punch this time, baby. Sabit knows revenge like a drunk knows an empty bottle, & I should have given up while I was ahead. *I've been wanting some new ink,* she says. *You helped me to finally make up my mind, that's all.* & before she can say anything else, I rip away the bandage. She does not even fucking flinch, even though the tattoo can't be more than a couple hrs old, still seeping & puffy and red, & all I can hear is her laughing. Bcause there on her back is the Roman numeral XVII, & when she asks for the bandage back, I slap her. I *slapped* her. This use of present tense, what's that but keeping the wound open & fresh, keeping the scabs at bay just like some goddamn pathetic stitchwork would do. I slapp*ed* her. The sound of my hand against her cheek was so loud, crack like a goddamn firecracker, & in the silence afterwards (just as fucking loud) she just smiled & smiled & smiled for me. & then I started yelling—I don't know exactly what—accusations that couldn't possibly have made sense, slurs and insinuation, and truthfully I knew even then none of it was anything but bitterness & disappointment that she'd not only managed to draw first blood (hahaha) this round, she'd finally pushed me far enough to hit her. I'd never hit her before. I had never hit *anyone* before, not since some bullshit highschool fights, &, at last, she did not even need to raise her voice. & then she just smiled @ me, & I think I must have finally told her to say something, bcause I was puking sick to death of that smug smile. *I'm glad you approve,* she said. Or maybe she said, *I'm glad you understand.* In this instance, the meanings would be the same somehow. Somehow interchangeable. But I did not apologize. That's the sort of prick I am. I sat down on the kitchen floor & stared @ linoleum patterns & when I looked up again she was gone. I don't know if she's *gone* gone, or if Sabit has merely retreated until she decides it's time for another blitz. Rethinking her maneuvers, the ins & outs of this campaign, logistics and field tactics & what the fuck ever. Cards must be played properly. I know Sabit, & she will never settle for Pyrrhic victory, no wars of attrition, no winner's curse. I sat on the floor until I heard the door shut & so knew I was alone again. I would say at least this gets me out of CeM on Sun. night, but I may go alone. Even though I know she'll be there. Clearly, I can hurt some more. Tonight I will get drunk, & that is all.

August 22, 2027 (2:56 a.m.)

Always have I been a sober drunk. I've finished the gin & started on an old bottle of rye whisky—gift from some former lover I won't name here—bcause I didn't feel like walking through the muggy, dusty evening, risking life and limb & lung for another pretty blue bottle of Bombay. A sober & lazy drunk, adverse to taking *unnecessary* risks. Sabit has not yet reappeared, likely she will not. I suspect she believes she has won not only the battle, but the war, as well. Good for her. May she go haunt some other sad fuck's life. Of course, the apt. is still awash in her junk, her clothes, her stitch lit, the hc zines and discs & her txtbooks filled with diagrams, schematics of skeletons & musculature, neuroanatomy, surgical technique, organic chem and pharmacology, immunology, all that crap. Snip porn. I should dump it all. I should call some-one 2830 to cart it all away so I don't have to fucking look at it anymore. The clothes, her lucite ashtrays, the smoky, musky, spicy smell of her, bottles of perfume, cosmetics, music, jewelry, deodor-ant, jasmine soap, & jesus all the *CRAP* she's left behind to keep me company. I don't know if I'll sleep tonight. I don't want to. I don't want to be awake anymore ever again. Why did she want to rub my nose in #17? Just that she's finally found a flaw, a goddamn weakness, & she has to make the most of it? A talkative, sober drunk. But wait—there is something. There is something else I found in Welleran Smith, & I'm gonna write it down. Something more from the diary/ies of Dr. Judith Darger, unless it's only something Smith concocted to suit his own ends. More & more I consider that likelihood, that Darger is only some lunatic just hap-pened to be where these people needed her to be, but isn't that how it always is with saints and martyrs? Questions of victimhood arise. Who's exploiting who? Whose exploiting whom? Christ I get lost in all these words. I don't *need* words. I'm strangling on words. I need to see Sabit & end this mess & be done with her. According to Welleran Smith, Darger writes (none of the "entries" are dated): "I would not tell a child that it isn't going to hurt. I wouldn't lie. It is going to hurt, and it is going to hurt forever or as long as human consciousness may endure. It is going to hurt until it doesn't hurt anymore. That is what I would tell a child. That is what I tell myself, and what am I but my own child? So, I will not lie to any of you. Yes, there will be pain, and at times the pain will seem unbearable. But the pain will open doorways. The pain *is* a doorway, as is the scalpel and as are the sutures and each and every incision. Pain is to be thrown open wide that all may gaze at the wonders which lie beyond. Why is it assumed this flesh must not be cut? Why is it assumed this is my final corporeal form? What is it we cannot yet see for all our fear of pain and ugliness and disfiguration? I would not tell a child that it isn't going to hurt. I would teach a child to live in pain." Is that what I am learning from you, Sabit? Is that the lesson of #17 and the glassy stare of those six eyes? Would you, all of you, teach me to live with pain?

August 23, 2027

It's almost dawn, that first false dawn & just a bit of hesitant purple where the sky isn't quite night anymore. As much as I have ever seen false dawn in the city, where we try so hard to keep the night away forever. If I had a son, or a daughter, I would tell them a story, how people are @ war with night, & the city—like all cities—is only a fortress built to hold back the night, even though all the world is just a bit of grit floating in a sea of night that might go on almost forever. I'm on the roof. I've never been up here before. Sabit & I never came up here. Maybe another three hours left before it's too hot & bright to sit up here, only 95F now if my watch is telling me the truth. My face & hair are slick with sweat, sweating out the booze & pills, sweating out the sour memory of Sabit. It feels good to sweat. I went to Pearl St. & the Trenton reveal @ *Corpus ex Machina*, but apparently she did not. Maybe she had something better to do & someone better to be doing it with. I flashed my press tag @ the door, so at least I didn't have to pay the $47 cover. I was not the only pundit in attendance. I saw Kline, who's over @ the Voice these days (that venerable old whore) & I saw Garrison, too. Buzzards w/their beaks sharp, stomach's empty, mouth's watering. No, I do not know if birds salivate, but reporters fucking do. None of them spoke to me, & I exchanged the favor. The place was *replete*, as the dollymops are wont to say, chock-full, standing room only. I sipped dirty martinis and licorice shides & looked no one in the eye, no one who was not on exhibit. #17 was near the back, not as well lit as some of the others, & I stood there & stared, bcause that is what I'd come for. Sometimes it gazed back @ me, or *they* gazed @ me—I am uncertain of the proper idiom or parlance or phrase. Is *it* One or are *they* 3? I stared & stared & stared, like any good voyeur would do, any dedicated peeper, bcause no clips are allowed, so you stand & drink it all in there the same way the Neanderthals did it or pony up the fat spool of cash for one of the Trenton chips or mnemonic lozenges ("all proceeds for R&D, promo, & ongoing medical expenses," of course). I looked until all I saw was all I was *meant* to see—the sculpted body(ies), living & breathing & conscious—the perpetually hurting realization of all Darger's nightmares. If I saw *beauty* there, it was no different from the beauty I saw in Brooklyn after the New Konsojaya Trading Co. popped their mini-nuke over on Tillary St. No different from the hundred lingering deaths I've witnessed. Welleran Smith said this was to be "the soul's terror- ism against the tyranny of genes & phenotype." I stood there & I saw everything there was to see. Maybe Sabit would have been proud. Maybe she would have been disappointed @ my resolve. It hardly matters, either way. A drop of sweat dissolving on my tongue & I wonder if that's the way the ocean used to taste, when it wasn't suicide to taste the ocean? When I had seen all I had come to see, my communion w/#17, I found an empty stool @ the bar. I thought you might still put in an appearance, Sabit, so I got drunker & waited for a glimpse of you in the crowd. & there was a man sitting next to me, Harvey somebody or another from Chicago, gray-haired with a mustache, & he talked & I listened, as best I could hear him over the music. I think the music was suffocating me. He said, *That's my granddaughter over there, what's left of her,* & he pointed thru the crush of bodies toward a stitchwork hanging from the warehouse ceiling, a dim chandelier of circuitry & bone & muscles flayed & rearranged. I'd looked at the piece on the way in—*The Lighthouse of Francis Bacon,* it was called. The old man told me he'd been following the show for months, but now he was almost broke & would have to head back to Chicago soon. He was only drinking ginger ale. I bought him a ginger ale & listened, leaning close so he didn't have to shout to be heard. The chandelier had once been a student @ the Pritzker School of Medicine, but then, he said, "something happened." I did not ask what. I decided if he wanted me to know, he would tell me. He didn't. Didn't tell me, I mean. He tried to buy me a drink, but I wouldn't let him. The grandfather of the Lighthouse of Francis Bacon tried to buy me a drink, & I realized I was thinking like a journalist again, *thinking you dumb fucks—here's your goddamn story—not some bullshit hearsay about chicanery among the snips, no, this old man's your goddamn story, this poor guy probably born way the fuck back before man even walked on the goddamn moon & now he's sitting here at the end of the world, this anonymous old man rubbing his bony shoulders with the tourists and art critics & stitch fiends and freaks because his granddaughter decided she'd rather be a fucking chandelier than a gynecologist.* Oh god, Sabit. If you could have shown *him* your brand-new tattoo. I left the place before midnight, paid the hack extra to go farther south, to get me as near the ruins as he dared. I needed to see them, that's all. Rings of flesh & towers of iron, right, rust-stained granite and the empty eye sockets where once were windows. The skyscraper stubs of Old Downtown, Wall St. and Battery Park City, all of it inundated by the rising waters there @ the confluence of the Hudson & the E. River. And then I came home, & now I am sitting here on the roof, getting less & less drunk, sweating & listening to traffic & the city waking up around me—the living fossil with her antique keyboard. If you *do* come back here, Sabit, if *that's* whatever happens next, you will not find me intimidated by your XVII or by #17, either, but I don't think you ever will. You've moved on. & if you send someone to pack up your shit, I'll probably already be in Bratislava by then. After CeM, there were 2 good assigns waiting for me in the green bin, & I'm taking the one that gets me far, far away from here for 3 weeks in Slovakia. But right now I'm just gonna sit here on the roof & watch the sun come up all swollen & lobster red over this rotten, drowning city, over this rotten fucking world. I think the pigeons are waking up.

Bradbury Weather

1.

I still have all the old books that Sailor left behind when she finally packed up and went looking for the Fenrir temples. I keep them in a big cargo crate with most of her other things, all that shit I haven't been able to part with. One of the books, a collection of proverbs, was written more than two hundred years ago by a Gyuto monk. It was published after his death in a Chinese prison, the manuscript smuggled out by someone or another, translated into Spanish and English, and then published in America. The monk, who did not wish to be remembered by name, wrote: "No story has a beginning, and no story has an end. Beginnings and endings may be conceived to serve a purpose, to serve a momentary and transient intent, but they are, in their truer nature, arbitrary and exist solely as a construct of the mind of man."

Sometimes, very late at night, or very early in the morning, when I should be sleeping or meditating, I read from Sailor's discarded books, and I've underlined that passage in red. If what I'm about to write down here needs an epigraph, that's probably as good as any I'll ever find, just as this beginning is as arbitrary and suitable as any I could ever choose. She left me. I couldn't have stopped her, not that I ever would have tried. I'm not that sort of woman. It was her decision, and I believed then it would have been wrong for me to interfere. But six months later, after the nightmares began, and I failed a routine mental-health evaluation, I resigned my teaching post and council seat and left to chase rumors and the ghost of her across the Xanthe Terra and Lunae Planum.

In Bhopai, a pornography dealer sold me a vid stick of Sailor dancing in a brothel. And I was told that maybe the stick had been made at Hope VII, a slatternly, backdust agradome that had seen better days and then some. I'd been up there once, on council business, more than twenty years before; Hope's Heaven, as the locals like to call the place, sits like a boil in the steep hills northwest of Tharsis Tholus. The dome has been breached and patched so many times it looks more like a quilt than a habitat.

I know a woman there. We worked together a few times, but that's ancient fucking history. These days, she runs a whorehouse, though everyone in Hope's Heaven calls her a mechanic, and who the hell am I to argue? Her bulls let me in the front door, despite my bureaucratic pedigree and the council brands on the backs on my hands. I played the stick for her, played it straight through twice, and Jun'ko Valenzuela shrugged her narrow, tattooed shoulders, shook her head once, and then went back to stuffing the bowl of her pipe with the skunky britch weed she used to buy cheap off the shiks down in New Riyadh.

I waited for her to finish, because I'd spent enough time in the mechanic's company to know that she talked when she was ready and fuck all if that wasn't good enough. If I got impatient, if I got pushy, she'd have one of her girls handing me my hat and hustling me straight back across town to the air station, no if's, and's, but's, or maybe's. So, I sat quietly in my chair and watched while she used an antique ivory tamper to get the weed just the way she wanted it, before lighting the pipe with a match. Jun'ko exhaled, and the smoke was the color of steel, almost the same color as her long dreadlocks.

"I don't do business with the law," she said. "Least ways, not if I have a choice. But you already *knew* that, didn't you, Dorry? You knew that before you came in here."

"I'm not police," I said, starting to feel like I was reading my lines from a script I'd rehearsed until the words had lost their meaning, going through motions designed to waste my time and amuse Jun'ko. "This isn't a criminal investigation," I assured her.

"It's bloody well close enough, *perra*. You're nothing but a bunch of goddamn witches, I say, badges or no badges, the whole lot of you Council rats."

"I don't work for any corporate agency or government corpus, nor do I—"

"Maybe not," she interrupted, "but you do work *with* them," and she squinted at me across the small table, her face wreathed in smoke. "Don't deny it. They say fuck, you ask who. You tell them whatever they need to know, whenever they come around asking questions, especially if there's a percentage for your troubles."

"I already told you, this is a personal matter. I told you that before I ran the stick."

"People tell me lots of things. Most times, turns out they're lying."

"Has it ever occurred to you that just might mean you're running in the wrong circles?" I asked, the question slipping out before I let myself think better of it. There she was trying to pick a fight, looking for any excuse to have me thrown out of her place, and there I was playing along, like I thought I'd ever get a second chance.

"Oh, the thought has crossed my mind," she said calmly around a mouthful of britch smoke, smiled, and the sinuous gold and crimson Chinese dragon tattooed on her left shoulder uncoiled and flashed its gilded eyes. "Why are you *asking* me if I've seen this little share crop of yours?" Jun'ko said, and she motioned at the vid stick with her pipe. "It's obvious that was scratched here, and nothing happens in my place I *don't* know about."

"Was she working for you?"

The dragon on her shoulder showed me teeth like daggers.

"Yeah, Dorry. She worked for me."

"When'd she leave?"

"I didn't say she had."

"But she's not here now—"

"No, she's not," Jun'ko Valenzuela said and stared into the softly glowing bowl of her pipe. "That one, she cashed out and bought herself a nook on a freighter that came through Heaven a couple months back. One of those big transpolar wagons, hauling ore down from the Acidalia."

"Did this freighter happen to have a name?"

"Oh, no damn doubt about it," she smiled and emptied the bowl of her pipe into an ashtray cut from cobalt-blue glass. "I just don't happen to remember what it was."

"Or where it was headed."

"Lots of places, most likely."

"She's looking for the Fenrir," I said, saying too much, and Jun'ko laughed and tapped her pipe against the edge of the ashtray.

"Jesus, Joseph, and Buddha, you know how to pick 'em, Dorry."

"She never told you that, that she was looking for the temples?"

"Hell, no. She kept to herself, mostly. And if I'd known she was hodging for the wolf, I'd never have put her skinny ass on the menu. *Mierda.* You listen to me, *cueca. Sácate el dedo del culo,* and you get yourself right the fuck back to Herschel City. Count yourself slick all this Jane cadged was your heart."

"Is that what you'd do, Jun'ko?"

She looked up at me, her hard brown eyes almost black in the dim light, and the dragon on her shoulder closed its mouth. "I got better sense than to crawl in bed with grey pilgrims," she said. "And you're officially out of time, Dorry. I trust you know the way back down to the street?"

"I think I can figure it out."

"That's cause you're such a goddamn smart lady. Of course, maybe you'd like to have a drink and sample the product first," and she nodded towards a couple of girls standing at the bar. "I'll even see you get a little discount, just to show there's no hard feelings."

"Thanks, but—"

"—she took your *huevos* with her when she left."

"I suppose that's one way of putting it," I replied, and she laughed again and began refilling her pipe.

"That's a goddamn shame," Jun'ko said and struck a match. "But you watch yourself out there. Way I hear it told, the Fenrir got more eyes than God. And they say he never sleeps."

When I stood up, she pointed at the two girls again. They were both watching me now, and one of them raised her skirt to show me that she had a dick. Jun'ko Valenzuela puffed at her pipe and shook her head. When she talked, smoke leaked from her mouth and from the jaws of the dragon tattoo. "Things ain't always what they seem. You don't forget that, Dorry. Not if you want to find this little *coño* and live to regret it."

The sun was already starting to slip behind Tharsis Tholus by the time I got back to the dingy, dusty sleeper that I'd rented near the eastern locks. The storm that had begun just before dawn still howled down the slopes of the great volcano, extinct two billion years if you trust the geologists, and battered the walls of Hope's Heaven, hammering the thin foil skin of the dome. I've always hated the western highlands, and part of me wanted nothing more than to take the mechanic's advice and go home. I imagined hauling the crate full of Sailor's belongings down the hall to the lift, pictured myself leaving it all piled on the street. It'd be easy, I told myself. It would be the easiest thing I'd ever done.

I ate, and, when the night came, I sat a little while in the darkness—I hadn't paid for electric—gazing out the sleeper's tiny window at the yellow runner lights dotting the avenue below, the street that led back up to Jun'ko's whorehouse or down to the docks, depending whether you turned left or turned right, north or south. When I finally went to bed, the nightmares found me, as they almost always do, and for a while, at least, I wasn't alone.

Just before dawn, I was awakened by a knock at the door, and I lay staring up into the gloom, looking for the ceiling, trying to recall where the hell I was and how I'd gotten myself there. Then I remembered smirking Jun'ko and her kinetitatts, and I remembered Hope VII, and then I remembered everything else. Whoever was out in the corridor knocked again, louder than before. I reached for my pants and vest, lying together on the floor near the foot of the cot.

"Who's there?" I shouted, hoping it was nothing more than someone banging on the wrong door, a drunk or an honest mistake. The only person in town whom I'd had business with was the mechanic, and as far as I was concerned, that business was finished.

"My name is Mikaela," the woman on the other side of the door called back. "I have information about Sailor. I may be able to help you find her. Please, open the door."

I paused, my vest still unfastened, my pants half on, half off. I realized that my mouth had gone dry, and my heart was racing. Maybe I'd pissed old Jun'ko off just a little more than I'd thought. Perhaps, in return, I was about to get the worst beating of my life, or perhaps word had gotten around the dome that the stranger from the east was an easy mark.

"Who sent you?" I asked, and when she didn't answer, I asked again. "Mikaela, *who* sent you here?"

"This would be easier, Councilor, if you'd open the door. I might have been followed."

"All the more reason for me to keep it shut," I told her, groping about in the dark for anything substantial enough to serve as a weapon, cursing myself for being too cheap to pay the five credits extra for electric.

"I'm one of the mechanic's girls," she said, almost whispering now, "but I swear she didn't send me. Please, there isn't time for this."

My right hand closed around an aluminum juice flask I'd bought in one of Heaven's market plazas the day before. It wasn't much, hardly better than nothing, but it'd have to do. I finished dressing, then crossed the tiny room and stood with my hand on the lockpad.

"I have a gun," I lied, just loud enough I was sure the woman would hear me.

"I don't," she replied. "Open the door. *Please.*"

I gripped the flask a little more tightly, took a deep breath, and punched in the twelve-digit security code. The door slid open immediately, whining on its rusty tracks, and the woman slipped past me while I was still half-blind and blinking at the flickering lamps set into the walls of the corridor.

"Shut the door," she said, and I did, then turned back to the darkened room, to the place where her voice was coming from. Yellow and white splotches drifted to and fro before my eyes, abstract fish in a lightless sea.

"Why is it so dark in here?" she asked, impatiently.

"Same reason I opened the door for you. I'm an idiot."

"Isn't there a window? All these nooks have windows," and I remembered that I'd closed and locked the shutters before going to bed, so the morning sun wouldn't wake me.

"There's a window, but you don't need to see me to explain why you're here," I said, figuring the darkness might at least even the odds if she were lying.

"Christ, you're a nervous nit."

"Why are you *here*?" I asked, trying to sound angry when I was mostly scared and disoriented, and took a step backwards, setting my shoulders squarely against the door.

"I told you. Sailor and me, we were sheba, until she paid off Jun'ko and headed south."

"South?" I asked. "The freighter was traveling south?"

"That's what she told me. Sailor, I mean. But, look here, Councilor, before I say any more, that quiff left owing me forty creds, and I'm not exactly in a position to play grace and let it slip."

"And what makes you think I'm in a position to pay off her debts, Mikaela? What makes you think I *would*?"

"You're a *titled* woman," she replied, and the tone in her voice made her feelings about the Council perfectly clear. "You've got it. And if you don't, you can get it. And you'll pay me, because nobody comes all the way the hell to Hope's Heaven looking for someone unless they want to find that someone awfully fucking bad. Am I wrong?"

"No," I sighed, because I didn't feel like arguing with her. "You're not wrong. But that doesn't mean you're telling the truth, either."

"About Sailor?"

"About anything."

"She told me about the Fenrir," the woman named Mikaela said. "It's almost all she ever talked about."

"That doesn't prove anything. That's nothing you couldn't have overheard at Jun'ko's yesterday evening."

Mikaela sighed. "I'm going to open the damned window," she said. "I hope you don't mind," and a moment later I heard her struggling with the bolt, heard it turning, and then the shutters spiraled open to reveal the easy, pinkish light of false dawn. Mikaela was prettier than I'd expected, and a little older. Her hair was pulled back in a long braid, and the light through the window revealed tiny wrinkles around her eyes. The face seemed familiar, and then I realized she was one of the women who'd been standing at the bar in Jun'ko's, the one who'd shown me that she had a penis. She sat down on the cot and pointed at the flask in my hand.

"Is *that* your gun?" she asked.

"I need to know whether or not you're telling me the truth," I said. "I don't think that's unreasonable, considering the circumstances."

"I'm a whore. That doesn't necessarily make me a thief and a liar."

"I need something, Mikaela."

"I'm actually a pretty good fuck," she said, as though it was exactly what I was waiting for her to say, and lay down on the cot. "You know, I'd wager I'm a skid better fuck than Sailor Li ever was. We could be sheba, you and me, Councilor. I'd go back to Herschel City with you, and you could forget all about her. If she wants to commit suicide, then, hell—"

"Something you couldn't have gotten from Jun'ko," I pressed. She rolled her eyes, which I could see were blue. There aren't many women on Mars with blue eyes.

"Yeah," she said, almost managing to sound disappointed, and clicked her tongue once against the roof of her mouth. "How's this? Sailor was with you for five years, if you count the three months after you started fucking her before you asked her to move into your flat. You lost two teeth in a fight when you were still just a kid, because someone called your birth mother an offworlder bitch, and sometimes the implants ache before a storm. The first time Sailor brought up the Fenrir, you showed her a stick from one of the containment crews and told her if she ever mentioned the temples again, you'd ask her to leave. When she *did* mention them again, you hit her so hard you almost—"

"You've made your point," I said, cutting her off. She smiled, a smug, satisfied smile, and nodded her head.

"I usually do, Dorry." She patted the edge of the cot with her left hand. "Why don't you come back to bed."

"I'm not going to fuck you," I replied and set the aluminum flask down on a shelf near the door. "I'll pay off whatever she owes you. You'll tell me what you know. But that's as far as it goes."

"Sure, if that's the way you want it." Mikaela shut her eyes. "Just thought I'd be polite and offer you a poke."

"You said the freighter was headed south."

"No. I said *Sailor* said it was headed south. And before I say more, I want half what I'm owed."

My eyes were beginning to adjust to the dim light getting in through the window, and I had no trouble locating the hook where I'd left my jacket hanging the night before. I removed my purse from an inside pocket, unfastened the clasp, and took out my credit tab. "How do you want to do this?" I asked, checking my balance, wondering how many more months I could make the dwindling sum last.

"Subdermal," she said. "Nobody out here carries around tabs, especially not whores."

I keyed in the amount, setting the exchange limit at twenty, and handed Mikaela the tab. She pressed it lightly to the inside of her left forearm, and the chip beneath her flesh subtracted twenty credits from my account. Then she handed the tab back to me, and I tried not to notice how warm it was.

"So, she told you the freighter was headed south," I said, anxious to have this over and done with and get this girl out of the sleeper.

"Yeah, that's what she said." Mikaela rolled over onto her right side, and her face was lost in the shadows. "The freighter's a Shimizu-Mochizuki ship, one of the old 500-meter ore buckets. You don't see many of those anymore. This one was hauling ice from a mine in the Chas Boreale to a refinery in Dry Lake, way the hell out on the Solis Planum."

"I know where Dry Lake is," I said, wondering how much of this she was inventing, and I sat down on the floor by the sleeper's door. "You've got an awfully good memory."

"Yes," she replied. "I do, don't I?"

"Do you also remember the freighter's name?"

"The *Oryoku Maru*, as a matter of fact."

"I can check these things out."

"I fully expect you to."

I watched her a minute or more, the angles and curves of her silhouette, wishing I had a pipe full of something strong, though I hadn't smoked in years. The shadows and thin wash of dawn between us seemed thicker than mere light and the absence of light.

"Does she know where she's going?" I asked, wishing I could have kept those words back.

"*She* thinks so. Anyhow, she heard there'd be a Fenrir priest on the freighter. She thought she could get it to talk with her."

"Why did she think that?"

"Sailor can be a very persuasive woman," Mikaela said and laughed. "Hell, I don't know. Ask her that when you find her."

"She thinks there's a temple somewhere on the Solis?"

"She wouldn't have told me that, and I never bothered to ask. I don't have the mark," and Mikaela held out her left arm for me to see. "She fucked me, and she liked to talk, but she's a pilgrim now, and I'm not."

"Did you try to stop her?"

"Not really. I told her she was fucking gowed, looking for salvation with that bunch of devils, but we're all free out here, Councilor. We choose our own fates."

Down on the street, something big roared and rattled past, its engines sounding just about ready for the scrap yard. Probably a harvester drone on its way to the locks and the fields beyond the dome. The sun was rising, and Hope VII was waking up around us.

"There's something else," Mikaela said, "something she wanted me to show you."

"She knew that I was coming?"

"She *hoped* you were coming. I should have hated her for that, but, like I said—"

"—you're all free out here."

"Bloody straight. Free as the goddamned dust," she replied. There was a little more light coming in the window now, morning starting to clear away the dregs of night, and I could see that Mikaela was smiling despite the bitterness in her voice.

"Did you want to go with her?"

"Are you fucking cocked? I wouldn't have gotten on that freighter with her for a million creds, not if she was right about there being a fucking Fenny priest aboard."

"So, what did she want you to show me?"

"Are you going after her?" Mikaela asked, ignoring my question, offering her own instead, and she sat up and turned her face towards the open window.

"Yes," I told her. "That's why I'm here."

"Then you *must* be cocked. You must be mad as a wind shrake."

"I'm starting to think so. What did she want you to show me, Mikaela."

"Most people call me Mickie," she said.

And I thought about paying her the other twenty and letting her go back to Jun'ko's or wherever it was she slept. There wasn't much of her street-smart bluster left, and it was easy enough to see that she was scared. It was just as easy to figure out why.

"My mum, she was a good Catholic," Mikaela said. "God, Baby Jesus, the Pope and St. Teresa, all that crap. And she used to tell me and my sisters that only the *evil* people have any cause to *fear* evil, but what'd she know? She never even left the dome where she was born. She never spent time out on the frontiers, never saw the crazy shit goes off out here. All the evil *she* ever imagined could be chased away with rosary beads and a few Hail Marys."

"Is it something you're afraid to show me, Mickie?" I asked, and she laughed and quickly hid her face in her hands. I didn't saying anything else for a while, just sat there with my back to the door of the sleeper, watching the world outside the window grow brighter by slow degrees, waiting until she stopped crying.

I wish I could say that Sailor had lied, or at least exaggerated, when she told Mikaela that I'd beaten her. I wish it with the last, stingy speck of my dignity, the last vestiges of my sense of self-loathing. But if what I'm writing down here is to be the truth, the truth as complete as I might render it, then that's one of the things I have to admit, to myself, to whoever might someday read this. To God, if I'm so unfortunate and the universe so dicked over that he or she or it actually exists.

So, yes, I beat her.

She'd been gone for several days, which wasn't unusual. She would do that sometimes, if we seemed to be wearing on one another. And it was mid-Pisces, deep into the long season of dust storms and endless wind, and we were both on edge. That time of year, just past the summer solstice, all of Herschel seems set on edge, the air ripe with static and raw nerves. I was busy with my duties at the university and, of course, with council business, and I doubt that I even took particular notice of her absence. I've never minded sleeping alone or taking my meals alone. If I missed her, then I missed the conversation, the sex, the simple contact with another human body.

She showed up just after dark one evening, and I could tell from the way she was dressed that she hadn't been at her mothers' or at the scholars' hostel near the north gate, the two places she usually went when we needed time apart. She was dirty, her hair coppery and stiff with dust, and she was wearing her heavy boots. So I guessed she'd been traveling outside the dome; maybe she'd taken the tunnel sled up to Gale or all the way down to Molesworth. I was in my study, going over notes for the next days lectures, and she came in and kissed me. Her lips were chapped and rough, faintly gritty, and I told her she needed a shower.

"Yeah, that'd be nice," she said. "If you stuck me right now, I think I'd bleed fucking dust."

"You were outside?" I asked, turning back to my desk. "That's very adventuresome of you."

"Did you miss me?"

"They've had me so busy, I hardly even noticed you were gone."

She laughed, the way she laughed whenever she wasn't sure that I was joking. Then I heard her unbuckling her boots, and afterwards she was quiet for a bit. Two or three minutes, maybe. When I glanced up, she'd taken off her gloves and rolled her right shirt sleeve up past the elbow.

"Don't be angry," she said. "Please."

"What are you on about now?" I asked, and then I saw the fevery red marks on the soft underside of her forearm. It might have only been a rash, except for the almost perfect octagon formed by the intersection of welts or the three violet pustules at the center of it all. I'd seen the mark before, and I knew exactly what it meant.

"At least hear me out," she said. "I had to know—"

"*What?*" I demanded, getting to my feet, pushing the chair roughly across the floor. "*What* precisely did you have to fucking *know*, Sailor?"

"If it's true. If there's something more—"

"More than what? Jesus fucking Christ. You let them touch you. You let those sick fucks *inside* of you."

"More than *this*," she said, retreating a step or two towards the doorway and the hall, retreating from me. "More than night and goddamn day. More than getting old and dying and no one even giving a shit that I was ever alive."

"How long's it been?" I asked, and she shook her head and flashed me a look like she didn't understand what I meant. "Since *contact*, Sailor. How long has it been since contact?"

"That doesn't matter. I wouldn't take the serum."

"We're not going to fucking argue about this. *Yes*, you're going to take the serum. We're going to the hospital right now, and you're going to start the serum *tonight*. If you're real bloody lucky, it might not be too late—"

"*Stop it!*" she hissed. "This isn't your decision, Dorry. It's my body. It's my goddamn life," and that's when she started crying. And that's when I hit her.

That's when I started hitting her.

There's no point pretending that I remember how many times I struck her. I only stopped when I saw the blood from her broken nose, splattered on the wall of my study. I like to believe that it wouldn't have happened if she hadn't started crying, those tears like a shield, like a weapon she'd fashioned from her weakness. I've always loathed the sight of tears, for no sane reason, and I like to think everything would have played out some other way if she just hadn't started crying. But that's probably bullshit, and even if it isn't, it wouldn't matter, would it? So, whatever I said earlier about not being the sort of woman to interfere in another's decisions, forget that. Remember this, instead.

Sailor left that night, and I haven't seen or heard from her since. I waited for a summons to appear before the quarter magistrate on charges of assault, but the summons never came, and one day I returned home from my morning classes, and most of her clothes were gone. I never found out if she retrieved them herself or if someone did it for her. A couple of weeks later, I learned that three Fenrir priests had been arrested near Kepler City, and that the district marshals suspected they'd passed near Molesworth and Herschel earlier in Pisces, that they'd been camped outside Mensae sometime back in Capricorn.

And that morning in Hope VII, all those months later, I sat and listened to Jun'ko's billygirl sobbing because she was afraid, and I dug my nails into my palms until the pain was all that mattered.

"I think you must miss her," Mikaela said, looking back over her left shoulder at me, answering a question I hadn't asked. "To have left Herschel and come all the way out here, to go poking around Jun'ko's place. Lady, no one comes to Heaven, not if she can help it."

"I've been here before," I said. "When I was young, about your age."

"Yeah, that's what Jun'ko was telling me," she replied, and I wanted to ask what else the mechanic might have told her, but I didn't. I was following Mikaela down a street so narrow it might as well have been an alleyway, three or four blocks over from the dome's main thoroughfare. Far above us, sensors buried in the framework of the central span were busy calibrating the skylights to match the rising sun outside. But some servo or relay-drive bot responsible for this sector of Hope VII had been down for the last few months, according to Mikaela. So we walked together in the lingering gloom, the patchy frost crunching softly beneath our feet, while the rest of the dome brightened and warmed. Once or twice, I noticed someone watching us through a smudgy window, suspicious eyes set in wary, indistinct faces, but there was no one on the street yet. The lack of traffic added to my unease and the general sense of desolation and decay; this was hardscrabble, even by the standards of Hope's Heaven. That far back from town center, almost everything was adobe brick and pressed sand-tile, mostly a jumble of warehouses, garages, and machine shops, with a shabby handful of old-line modular residential structures stacked about here and there. If Mikaela was leading me into an ambush, she couldn't have chosen a better setting.

"You hang close to me, Councilor," she said. "People around here, they don't care so much for outsiders. It's a bad part of town."

"You mean to say there's a *good* part?" I asked, and she laughed, then stopped and peered down a cross street, rubbing her hands together for warmth. Her breath steamed in the morning air.

"No," she said. "I sure wouldn't go so far as to say that. But there's bad and there's worse." She frowned and looked back the way we'd come.

"Is something wrong?" I asked. She shook her head, then pointed east, towards the cross street.

"It's that way, just a little piece farther," she said, and then she changed the subject. "Is it true you've been offworld? That's what Jun'ko said, that you've been up to Eos Station, that you've seen men. Men from Earth."

I nodded my head, still looking in the direction she'd pointed. "It's true. But that was a long time ago."

"What were they like?" she asked, and I shrugged.

"Different," I replied, "but not half so different as most of us think. Two eyes, two hands, one mouth, a dick," and I jabbed a thumb at her skirt. "More like some of us than others."

It was a crude comment, one I never would have made if I hadn't been so nervous, and I half expected her to blush or get pissed or something. But Mikaela only kicked at a loose paving tile and rubbed her hands together a little harder, a little faster.

"Yeah, well, that was Jun'ko's idea," she said. "She even paid the surgeon. Claimed I wasn't pretty enough, that I needed something special, you know, something exotic, if I was gonna work out of her place. It's not so bad. Like I said, I'm a pretty good fuck. Better than I was before."

"No regrets, then?"

She made a half-amused, snorting noise, wiped her nose on the sleeve of her jacket, and stared at her shoes. "I was born here," she said. "What the hell would I do with a thing like regret?"

"When are you going to tell me what's waiting for me down there, Mickie?" I asked, and she almost smiled.

"Sailor said you'd be like this."

"Like what?"

"She said you weren't a very trusting person. She said you had a nasty habit of stabbing people in the back before they could beat you to it."

I suppose that was payback for the remark about her penis, nothing I didn't have coming, but it made me want to slap her. Before I could think of a reply, she was moving again, walking quickly away from me down the side street. I thought about turning around and heading straight back to the station. It was still three long hours until the next zep, but I could try to get a secure uplink and see what there was to learn about the *Oryoku Maru*. Following the whore seemed like a lazy way to commit suicide.

I followed her, anyway.

A couple of minutes later, we ducked through a low archway into what appeared to be an abandoned repair shop. It was dark inside, almost too dark to see, and even colder than it had been out on the street. The air stank of spent engine oil and hydrosol, dust and mildew and rat shit, and the place was crowded with the disassembled, rusting skeletons of harvesters and harrow rigs. They loomed around us and hung from ceiling hoists, broken, forgotten beasts with sickle teeth.

"Watch your step, Councilor," Mikaela warned, calling back to me after I tripped over some piece of machinery or another and almost stumbled into an open garage pit. I paused long enough to catch my breath, long enough to whisper a thankful prayer and be sure I hadn't broken my ankle.

"We need a fucking torch," I muttered, my voice much louder than I'd expected, magnified and thrown back at me by the darkness pressing in around us.

"Well, I don't have one," she said, "so you'll just have to be more careful."

She took my hand and guided me out of the repair bay, along a pitch-black corridor that turned left, then right, then left again, before finally ending in a dim pool of light spilling in through a number of ragged, fist-sized holes in the roof. I imagined it was sunlight, though it wasn't, of course, imagined it was warm against my upturned face, though it wasn't that, either.

"Down here," she said, and I turned towards her voice, blinking back orange and violet afterimages. We were standing at the top of a stairwell.

"I hid it when Sailor left," Mikaela said. "Jun'ko has our rooms tossed once or twice a month, regular as clockwork, so I couldn't leave it in the house. But I figured it'd be safe here. When I was a kid, my sister and I used to play hide-and-seek in this place."

"You have a sister?" I asked, and she started down the stairs without me, taking them two at a time despite the dark. I hurried to catch up, more afraid of being left alone in this place than wherever she might be leading me.

"Yeah," she called back. "I've got a little sister. She's out there somewhere. Sheba'd up with a guild mason down in Arsia Mons, last I heard. But we don't talk much these days. She got sick on Allah and doesn't approve of whoring anymore."

We reached the bottom of the stairs, and I glanced back up at the patch of imitation daylight we'd left at the top. "How much farther, Mickie?" I asked, trying hard to sound calm, trying to sound confident, trying desperately to bury my anxiety in a pantomime of equipoise. But the darkness was quickly becoming more than I could handle, so much darkness crammed into the gap between the walls and floor and ceiling. It was becoming inconceivable that this place might somehow simultaneously contain so much darkness and ourselves. *I'm a little claustrophobic,* I pretended to have said, so that the mechanic's girl would understand and get this the hell over and done with. Past the bottom of the stairs, the air was damp and smelled of mold and stagnant water, mushrooms and rotting cardboard. I was sweating now, despite the cold.

"She made me promise that I'd keep it safe," Mikaela said, as if she hadn't heard my question or had simply chosen to ignore it. "I'm not really used to people trusting me with things. Not with things that matter to—"

"How much *farther*?" I asked again, more insistent than before. "We need to hurry this up, or I'll miss my flight."

"Here," she said. "Right there, on your left," and when I turned my head that way, there was the faintest chartreuse glow, like some natural phosphorescence, a glow that I could have sworn hadn't been there just a few seconds before. "Just inside the doorway, on the table," Mikaela said.

I took a deep breath of the fetid air and stepped past her through an opening leading into what might once have been a storeroom or maintenance locker. The glow became much brighter than it had been out in the corridor, illuminating the bare concrete walls, an M5 proctor droid that had been stripped raw and left for dead, the intestine tangle of sagging pipes above my head. The yellow-green light was coming from a five- or six-liter translucent plastic catch cylinder, something that had probably been manufactured as part of a dew-farm's cistern. And I stood staring at the pale thing floating inside the cylinder—not precisely dead because it had probably never been precisely alive—a wad of hair and mottled flesh, bone and the scabby shell of a half-formed exoskeleton.

"She said it was yours, Dorry," Mikaela whispered from somewhere behind me. "She said she didn't know, when she took the mark, didn't know she was pregnant."

I said something. I honestly can't remember what.

It hardly matters.

The thing in the cylinder twitched and opened what I hadn't realized was an eye. It was all pupil, that eye, and blacker than space.

"She lost it before she even got here," the whore said, "when she was working up in Sytinskakya. She couldn't have taken it with her to the temples, and I promised her that I'd keep it safe. She thought you might want to take it back with you."

I turned away from the unborn thing, which might or might not have seen my face, pushing my way roughly past Mikaela and back out into the corridor. The darkness there seemed almost kind after the light from the catch cylinder, and I let it swallow me whole as I ran. I only fell twice or maybe three times, tripping over my own feet and sprawling hard on sand-tile or steel, then right back up in an instant, blindly making my way to the stairwell and the cluttered repair shop above, and, finally, to the perpetually shadowed street. I stopped and looked back then, breathless and faint and sick to my belly, pausing only long enough to see that Jun'ko's girl hadn't followed me. By the time I reached the transfer station at the lower end of Avenue South Eight, the morning was fading towards noon, and what I'd seen below Hope's Heaven seemed hardly as substantial, hardly as thinkable, as any woman's guilty dreams of Hell.

I have Sailor's book of proverbs from the cargo crate open on the table in front of me, the one written by the 21st-Century Tibetan monk. There's a passage here on dreams, one of the passages I've underlined in red, which reads, "The pathway to Nirvana is a road along which the traveler penetrates the countless illusions of his waking mind, his dreams and dreamless sleep. There must be a full and final awakening from all illusion, waking and dreaming. By many forms of meditation a man may at last achieve this necessary process of waking up in his life and in his dreams and nightmares. He may follow Vipassanâ in search of lasting, uninterrupted self-awareness, finally catching himself in the very act of losing himself in the cacophonous labyrinth of his thoughts and fantasies and the obscuring tides of emotion and sexual impulse that work to impede awakening."

I like to think that I know what most of that means, but, then again, I'm an arrogant woman, and admitting ignorance galls me. I may not have the faintest clue.

On the long flight from Hope VII, from the ages-dead caldera of Tharsis Tholus towards the greater, but equally spent, craters of Pavonis Mons and Arsia Mons, skirting the sheer, narrow fissures of the Noctis Fossae and the dismal mining operations scattered like old scabs out along the edges of that district, as the zep drifted high above the rust-colored world, I dozed, losing myself in those obscuring tides. It's not the same dream every time. I'm not sure I believe in dreams which recur with such absolute perfection that they're always the same dream. So, then, this is a collective caricature of the dreams that I've had since Sailor left, an approximation of the dream I must have had as the drone of the zep's engines answered my exhaustion and dragged me down to sleep.

I'm standing outside the vast, impenetrable dome of Herschel City, locked safely inside my pressure suit, breathing clean, fresh air untainted by the fine red dust blowing down from Elysium. I can hear the wind through my comms, wild and terrible as any mythological banshee long since exiled here from Earth. In the distance, far across the plain, I can see a procession, a single-file line of robed figures and their cragged assortment of sandrovers and skidwagons. A great cloud of dust rises up behind them and hangs like a caul, despite the wind. *Impervious* to the wind. And I am filled with such complete dread, a fear like none that I have never known, but I take one step forward. There's music coming through my helmet, flutes and violins and the thump-thump-thump of drums. I know that music at once, though I've never heard it before. I know that music instinctively.

"They're not for you, Dorry," Sailor says, and I turn, turning my back on the procession, and she's standing there with her left hand on the shoulder of my suit. She isn't wearing one herself. She isn't wearing much of anything, and the dust has painted her skin muted shades of terra-cotta. She might be another race entirely, another species, something alien or angelic or ghostly that I have fucked and loved thinking she was only a human girl.

"They would never let you follow," she says. "Not as you are now."

I don't wonder how she can breathe, or how her body is enduring the bitter cold or the low pressure. I only want to hold her, because it's been so long, and I never imagined I would really see her again. But then she pushes me away, frowning, that look she used to get whenever she thought I was being particularly stupid. She licks her red-brown lips, and her tongue is violet.

"No," she says, sounding almost angry, almost hateful. "You *hit* me, Dorry. And I don't need that shit. If I needed that shit, I'd have stayed with fucking Erin Antimisiaris. If I needed to be someone's punch hound, I'd go hunt up my asshole swap-mother and let *her* have another go at me."

She says other, more condemning things, and I say nothing at all in my defense, because I *know* she's telling the truth, laying it all out for me as the sun crawls feebly across the wide china sky. And then, slowly, grain by grain, the wind takes her apart, weathers her away until her face is hardly recognizable, a statue that might have stood at this spot a thousand years; her body has begun to crumble, too, reclaimed by the ground beneath our feet. I turn once more towards the procession, but it has passed beyond the range of my vision.

And then we are lying in my bed, and the air smells like fresh cinnamon and clean linen, a musky, faint hint of sweat and sex, and Sailor lights her pipe. I wonder how long I've been sleeping, how long the dream could have lasted, and as I turn to tell her about it all—an act of sharing secrets to rob the nightmare of its claws—the room dissolves around me, and I'm standing alone at the edge of a crater so wide I can see only a little ways across it. I'm facing west, I think, and the sky is a roiling kaleidoscope of clotted, oily grays and blues, blacks and deep purples, no sky that any women has ever seen on Mars. *That's the color of nausea*, I think. *That's the color of plague and decay.*

I hear the music again, then. The pipes. The bows drawn across taut strings. The drums sounding out loudly across the flat, monotonous floor of the impact crater. A billion years ago, something fell screaming from the sky and buried itself here, broke apart in a storm of fire and vaporized stone, and here it has been waiting. It was here when the progenitors of humankind were mere protoplasmic slime clinging desperately to the sanctuary of abyssal hydrothermal vents. It was waiting when our australopithecine foremothers first looked up and noticed the red star hanging above African skies. It was here when men finally began to send their probes and landers, waiting while the human invasion was planned and executed. But not waiting patiently, because nothing so burned and shattered and hungry can wait patiently, but waiting all the same, because it has been left no choice. It has been cast down, gravity's prisoner, and I look back once, looking back at the wastes stretching out behind me, before I begin the long, painful climb down to the place where the music is coming from.

2.

I was having a bowl of sage tea, the strong stuff the airlines serve, when I first noticed the journalist. She was sitting across the aisle from me, a few rows nearer the front of the passenger cabin, and she made no attempt to hide the fact that she was watching me. Her red hair was tied back in the high, braided topknot that had become so fashionable in the eastern cities, held up with an elaborate array of hematite and onyx pins. She was wearing a stiff brown MBS uniform, and when she saw me looking at her, she nodded and stood up.

"Fuck me," I muttered and then turned to stare out the portal, through thin, hazy clouds at the barren landscape fifteen hundred feet below the zep. We'd already made the stop at the new Keeslar-Nguyen depot near Arsia Mons and, afterwards, the airship had turned east, heading out across the Solis Planum.

"May I sit with you, Councilor?" the journalist asked a few moments later, and when I looked up, she was pointing at the empty seat opposite me. She was smiling, that practiced smile to match the casual tone of her voice, all of it meant to put me at ease and none of it doing anything of the sort.

"Do I really have any say in the matter?"

Her smile almost faded, not quite, but it faltered just enough that I could see that she was nervous, her confidence a thin act, and I wondered just how long it had been since the net had given this one her implants and press docs and sent her off into the world. I think I was even a little insulted that I didn't rate someone more experienced.

"You must have known I was coming," she said, her voice not quite quavering. "You must have known *someone* would come."

"I know I'm going to die one day, and I'm not so happy about that, either."

"Why don't we skip this part, Councilor?" she asked, sitting down. "I'm just doing my job. I only want to ask you a few questions."

"Even though you know ahead of time that I don't want to answer them." I sipped at my tea, which was growing cold, and looked out the portal again.

"Yes. Something like that," she replied, and I knew that the cameras floating on her corneas, jacked into her forebrain and the MBS satellites, were relaying every word that passed between us, every move I made, to the network's clearcast facilities in Herschel. The footage would be trawled, filtered, and edited as we spoke and broadcast seconds after our conversation ended.

"Have you ever been out this far?" I asked.

"No," she said, and I allowed myself to be impressed that the question hadn't thrown her. "Before this jaunt, I've never been any farther west than the foundries at Ma'adim Vallis."

"And how are you liking it so far, the frontiers?"

"It's big," she said, and cleared her throat. "Too damned big."

I drank the last of my tea and set the bowl down on the empty seat to my right; one of the attendants would be along soon to take it away.

"You were at that whorehouse in Hope VII," she said, "looking for your lover, Sailor Li."

"Is that so? Tell me, whoever the hell you are, is this what's passing for investigative work at MBS these days?" I asked and laughed. It felt good to laugh, and I tried to remember the last time I'd done it. I couldn't.

"My name is Ariadne," she said, and sighed. "Ariadne Vaughn. You know, it might be in your best interest to try not to be such an asshole."

"And why is that, Ariadne?"

She stared at me a long second or two, then rubbed hard at the bridge of her nose like maybe it had started to itch. She sighed again and glanced at the portal. She couldn't have been much older than thirty, thirty-five at the outside, and I realized I wanted to fuck her. I suppose that should have elicited in me some sort of shame or disgust with myself, but it didn't.

"I asked you a simple question, Ariadne. Why might it be in my best interest not to be such an asshole."

"Because I might know where Sailor is," she said. "All we want is the story. You're the first council member known to have involvement with the Fenrir. Answer a few questions, and I'll tell you what I know."

My mouth had gone dry, and I wished I had another bowl of the hot, too-strong tea. "Sailor's the pilgrim here," I told the journalist, "not me. If you think otherwise, you're sorely mistaken."

"The way the network sees it, if your lover's chasing the wolf and *you're* chasing your lover, that places you pretty damned close to—"

"I can have you put off at the next port," I said, interrupting her. "I still have that much authority."

"And how's that going to look, Councilor?" she asked, beginning to sound more confident now, and she leaned towards me and lowered her voice. I caught the sour-sweet scent of slake on her breath and realized why she'd been rubbing her nose. "I mean, unless this little walkabout of yours is some sort of suicide slag," she said, almost whispering.

"You're a junky," I replied, as indifferently, as matter-of-factly, as I could manage. "Does the network buy it for you, the slake? With that much circuitry in your skull, I know *they* must know you're dragging."

Ariadne Vaughn blinked her left eye, shutting down the feed.

"I'm just wondering how it all works out," I continued. "Does the MBS have a special arrangement with the cops to protect junky remotes from prosecution?"

"They warned me you were a cunt," she said.

"They did their homework. Good for them."

She didn't say anything for a minute or two. One of the attendants came by, took my empty bowl, and I ordered another, this time with a shot of brandy.

"Are you lying to me about Sailor?" I asked the journalist, and she narrowed her dark eyes, eyes the color of polished agate, then shook her head and tried to look offended. "Because if you *are*," I said, "after what I've been through and seen the past eight months, you ought to understand that I'd have no problem whatsoever with making a few calls that'll land you in flush so fast you won't even have time for one last fix before they plug you into detox." I stabbed an index finger at her nostrils, and she flinched.

"That's a fact, little girl. You fuck me on this, and once the plumbers are finished, there won't be enough of you left for the network gats to bother salvaging the hardware. Are we absolutely clear?"

"Yes, Councilor," she said very softly, rubbing at her nose again. "I understand you very well."

I looked down the long aisle towards the zeppelin's small kitchen, wishing the attendant would hurry up with my tea and brandy. "Then ask me your questions, Ariadne Vaughn," and I glanced at my watch. "You have ten minutes."

"Ten *minutes?*" she balked. "No, Councilor, I'm afraid I'll need quite a bit more than that if—"

"Nine minutes and fifty-four seconds," I replied, and she nodded and blinked her agate-colored camera eyes on again.

Sometimes, in the dreams, I actually reach the floor of the crater. And I see it all with such clarity, a clarity that doesn't fade upon waking, a clarity such that I have sometimes been tempted to identify the crater as a real place, existing beyond the limits of my recurring nightmares. I take down a chart or my big globe and put a finger *there*, or *there*, or *there*. It might be Lomonosov, far out and alone on the Vastitas Borealis. Or it might be Kunowsky farther to the south, smaller, but just as desolate. I was once almost certain that it was the vast, weathered scar of Huygens. No one ever goes there, that pockmarked wasteland laid out above the dead inland sea of the Hellas Planitia. Not even the prospectors and dirt mags make it that far west, and if they do, they don't make it back. Anything at all might be hiding in a place like that. *Anything.* But I know that it *isn't* Huygens, and it isn't Lomonosov or Kunowsky, either, and, in the end, I always set the globe back in its place on my shelf and return the charts to their drawers.

Sometimes, I make it all the way down to the bottom.

The music rises and swells around me like a dust storm, like *all* the dust storms that have ever scrubbed the raw face of this godforsaken planet. I stand there, wrapped in a suffocating melody that is almost cacophony, melody to drown me, trying to remember where I've heard this music before, knowing only that I have. I gaze back up at the rim of the crater, so sharp against the star-filled night sky, and trace my footprints and the displaced stones and tiny avalanches that mark the zigzag path of my descent.

I know full well that I'm being watched—some vestigial, primitive lobe of my brain pricked by that needling music, pricked by a thousand alien eyes—and I turn and begin the long march into the crater, towards its distant central peak and the place where the music might be coming from. I know that she's out there somewhere—Sailor—not waiting for me. I know that she's already given herself over to the Fenrir, and that means she's something worse than dead now. But I also know that doesn't mean I'm not supposed to find her.

The sky is full of demons.

Blood falls from Heaven.

I was sent to the containment facility just north of Apollinaris Patera only three months after my election to the Council. On all the fedstat grids it's marked as IHF21, a red biohazard symbol at Latitude -9.8, Longitude 174.4E to scar the northern slope of the volcano. But the physicians and epidemiologists, virologists and exobiologists and healers who work and live there call it something else, something I'd rather not write down just now. The patients or detainees or whatever you might choose to call them, if *they* have a name for the place, then I've never learned it. I'd never want to.

That was seventeen years ago, not long after a pharmaceutical multinational working with the Asian umbrella came up with the serum, the toxic antiviral cocktail that either kills you or slows down the contagion and sometimes even stops it cold, but never reverses the alterations already made to the genome of the infected individual. So, there was something like hope in IHF21 when I arrived. That is, there was hope among the staff, not the inmates, who were each and every one being administered the serum against their will. The scientists reasoned that if a serum that inhibited the Fenrir contagion had been found, a genuine cure might not be far behind it. But by the time I left, almost four years later, with no cure in sight and a resistance to the serum manifesting in some of the infected, that hope had been replaced by something a lot more like resignation.

The blood from Heaven is black and hisses when it strikes the hard, dusty ground. I step over and around the accumulated carcasses of creatures I know no names for, the hulks of other things I'm not even sure were ever alive. Corpses that might have belonged to organisms or machines or some perverse amalgam of the two. With every step, the plain before me seems ever more littered with these bodies, if they are, indeed, dead things. Some of them are so enormous that I step easily between ebony ribs and follow hallways roofed by fossilized vertebrae and scales like the hull plating of starships. The music is growing louder, yet through it I can hear the whisperers, the mumbling phantoms that I've never once glimpsed.

Three days after I arrived at IHF21, a senior physician, an earthborn woman named Zyra McNamara, led me on a tour of the Primary Ward, where the least advanced cases were being tended. The *least* advanced cases. There was hardly anything human left among them. I spent the better part of half an hour in a lavatory, puking up my lunch and breakfast and anything else that would come. Then I sat with Dr. McNamara in a staff lounge, a small room with a view of the mountain, sipping sour, hot coffee and listening to her talk.

"Is it true that they're not dying?" I asked, and she shrugged her shoulders.

"Yes. Strictly speaking, it's true that no one's died of the contagion, so far. But, you have to understand, we're dealing with such fundamental questions of organismal integrity—" and then she paused to stare out the window for a moment. There was a strong wind from the east, and it howled around the low plastic tower that held the lounge, rattled the windowpane, roared around the ancient ash and lava dome of Apollinaris Patera rising more than five kilometers above datum.

"It's now my belief," she said, "that we have to stop thinking of this thing as a disease. If I'm right, it's really much more like a parasite. Or rather, it's a viroid that reduces its victims to obligate parasites." And she was silent for a moment then, as though giving me a chance to reply or ask a question. When I didn't, much too busy trying to calm my stomach for questions, she went on.

"On Earth, there are a number of species of fish that live in the deepest parts of the oceans. They're commonly, collectively, called anglerfish, and in these anglerfish, the males are very much smaller than the females. The males manage to locate the female fish in total darkness by honing in on the light from bioluminescent organs which the females possess."

"We're talking about *fish?*" I asked. "After what you just showed me, those things lying in there, we're sitting here talking about fucking fish?"

Dr. McNamara took a deep breath and let it out slowly. "Yes, Councilor. We're talking about fish. You see, the males begin their lives as autonomous organisms, but when they finally locate a female, which must be an almost impossible task given the environmental conditions involved, they attach themselves to her body with their jaws and become parasitic. In time, they completely fuse with the female's body, losing much of their skeletal structure, sharing a common circulatory system, becoming, in essence, no more than reproductive organs. The question is, do the males, in some sense, *die?* They can no longer live free of the host female. They receive all of their nutrients via her bloodstream—"

"I don't understand what you're saying," I told her, and looked down at the floor between my feet, starting to think I was going to vomit again.

"Don't worry about it, Councilor. We'll talk again later, when you're feeling better. There's no hurry."

There's no hurry.

But in my dreams, as I make my way across that corpse-strewn crater, my head and lungs and soul filled to bursting with the Fenrir's music, I am seized by an urgency beyond anything that I've ever known before. My feet cannot move quickly enough, and, after a while, I realize that it's not even Sailor that I'm looking for, not her that I'm navigating this terrible, impossible graveyard to find.

I have never reached the center.

I have never reached the center yet.

Since I was a child, I've loved the zeps. When I was four or five, my mothers took me to the Carver Street transfer station, and we watched together as one enormous gray airship docked and another departed. There was even a time when I fantasized that I might someday become a pilot, or an engineer. I read books on general aerodynamics and the development of Martian zeps, technical manuals on hybrid tricyclohydrazine/solar fuel cells and prop configuration and the problems of achieving low-speed lift in a thin, CO_2-heavy atmosphere. I built plastic models that my mothers had bought for me in Earthgoods shops. And then, at some point, I moved on to other, less-remarkable things. Puberty. Girls. And my mathematics and low-grade psi aptitude scores that eventually led to my seat on the Council. But I still love the zeps, and I love traveling on them. They are elegant things in a world where we have created very little elegance and much ugliness. They drift regally above Mars like strange helium-filled animals, almost like the gigantic floaters that evolved almost three hundred and fifty million miles away in the Jovian atmosphere. I'd been praying that the long flight from Hope VII to the military port at the eastern edge of the Claritas Fossae might be some small relief after the horror that Jun'ko's billygirl had shown me. But first there'd been the nightmare, and now this network *mesuinu* and her camera eyes and questions I'd agreed to hear.

"How do you spell 'anglerfish'?" she asked, scribbling something on a pad she'd pulled from the breast pocket of her brown jacket.

"*What?*"

"Anglerfish. Is it one word or two? I've never heard it before."

"How the hell would I know? What the fuck difference does it make? You're doing this on short delay, right?"

She frowned and wrote something on the pad. It was somehow sickeningly quaint, watching a cyborg with an eight-petabyte recall chip making handwritten notes.

"Do you think you'll forget?" I asked and sipped my second

bowl of tea. The brandy was strong and better than I'd expected, the steam from the tea filling my head and making Ariadne Vaughn's questions a little easier to endure.

She laughed and thumped the pad with one end of her stylus. 'Oh, that. It's just an old habit. I don't think I'll ever quite get over it."

"I don't know how to spell 'anglerfish'," I lied.

"Jun'ko Valenzuela told me that you were trailing a freighter, that one of her girls said Sailor Li had booked passage on a freighter named *Oryoku Maru*."

"How much did you have to pay her to tell you that?" I asked. "Or did you find that threats were more effective with Jun'ko?"

"Are there currently any plans to allow civilian press into the containment facilities?"

"No," I said, watching her over the rim of my bowl. "The Council's public affairs office could have told you that."

"They did," she replied. "But I wanted to hear it from you. Now, there are rumors that you physically abused Sailor Li before she left you. Is that true, Councilor?"

I didn't answer right away. I sipped at my tea, glaring at her through the steam, trying to grasp the logic behind her seemingly random list of questions. The progression from one topic to another escaped me, and I wondered if something in her head was malfunctioning.

"Councilor, did you ever *beat* your lover?" she asked again and chewed at her lower lip.

I thought about lying, and then I said, "I hit her."

"After she took the mark?"

"Yes. I hit her after she took the mark."

"But no charges were ever filed with the magistrate's office in Herschel. Why do you think that is?"

I smiled and set my bowl down on the portal ledge. Vibrations through the wall of the airship sent tiny concentric ripples across the surface of the dark liquid.

"There have been allegations that the Council saw to it that no charges were filed against you," the journalist said. "Are you aware of that?"

"Sailor never brought charges against me because she knew if the case went to trial that I'd confess, and if I were in jail, I couldn't follow her. And, besides, she didn't have time left to waste on trials, Ms. Vaughn. She had more pressing matters to attend to."

"You mean the Fenrir?"

"No, Ms. Vaughn, I mean making a fortune as a whore in Hope VII."

She laughed, the comfortable sort of laugh she might have laughed if we were old, close friends and what I'd just said was no more than a joke. Once, not long after I returned to Herschel City from IHF21, one of the members of the Council's Board of Review and Advancement told me that she was deeply disturbed at my cynicism, my propensity for hatred, and that I was so quick to judge and anger. I admitted the fault and promised to meditate twice daily towards freeing myself of these shortcomings. I might as well have promised to raise the dead or make Mars safe for the XY chromo crowd. And now, sitting there on the *Barsoom XI*, facing this woman for whom my life and Sailor's life and the Fenrir contagion were together no more than a chance for early promotion and a fat bonus from the network snigs, I realized that I cherished my ability to hate. I cherished it as surely as I'd cherished Sailor. As surely as I'd once stood in the shadows of docking zeppelins, joyful and dizzy with the bottomless wonder of childhood.

I could have killed the smiling bitch then and there, could have slammed her head against the aluminum-epoxy alloy wall of the zep's cabin until there was nothing left to shatter, and my fingers were slick and sticky with her blood and brains and the yellowish lube and cooling fluids of her ruptured optical and super-palatal implants.

I could have done it in an instant, with no regrets. But there was still Sailor and the Fenrir's music, that beckoning anglerfish bioluminescence shining brightly through absolute blackness and cold, leading me to a different and more unthinkable end than the sanctuary of a prison cell.

"Do you really think you'll find her?" Ariadne Vaughn asked.

"If I live long enough," I replied, turning to the portal again. The sun was beginning to set.

"There are rumors, Councilor, that you've already been infected, that the contagion was passed to you by Sailor."

I slowly, noncommittally, nodded my head for her, for everyone at MBS studios and everyone who would soon be seeing this footage, and watched as the western sky turned the color of bruises. I didn't bother telling her what she already knew, repeating data stored in her pretty patchwork skull, that the viroid can only be contracted directly from specialized delivery glands inside the cloaca of a Fenrir drone. The infected aren't contagious. She knew that.

"That's fifteen," I said instead, glancing from the portal to my watch, even though it had actually been more like twenty minutes since she'd started asking me questions. "Time's all up."

"Well then, we wish you luck," she said, mock cheerfully, ending the rambling interview, "and Godspeed in your return to Herschel City."

"Bullshit," I said quickly, before she had a chance to blink the o-feed down. She frowned and shook her head.

"You know that's going to be edited out," she said, returning the pad and stylus to her breast pocket. "You *know* that, Councilor."

"Yeah, I know that. But it felt good, anyway. Now, Ms. Vaughn, you tell me where you think she is," I said and smiled at the flight attendant as she passed our seats.

"I assume you've had a look at the *Oryoku Maru*'s route db," she said, rubbing at her itching nose again. I wondered how long it would be before the slake necessitated reconstructive rhinoplasty, or, if perhaps, it already had. "So you know it's last refueling stop before the south polar crossing is at Lowell Station."

"Yes," I told her. "I know that. But I don't think Sailor will go that far. I think she'll get off before Lowell. I'm guessing Bosporos."

"Then you're guessing wrong, Councilor."

"And just what the hell makes you think that?" I asked. Ariadne Vaughn cocked her head ever so slightly to one side, raised her left eyebrow, and I imagined her rehearsing this moment in front of mirrors and prompts and vidloops, working to get that ah-see-this-is-what-I-know-that-you-*don't* expression just exactly fucking right. I began to suspect there were other cameras planted in the zep, that we were still being pixed for MBS. "There's nothing in Lowell. There hasn't been since the war."

"We have some reliable contacts in the manifest dep and hanger crews down there," she replied, leaning back in her seat, either putting distance between us or playing out another part of the pantomime. "The last couple of years, Fenrir cultists have been moving in, occupying the old federal complex and some of the adjacent buildings. All the company people stay away from the place, of course, but they've seen some things. Some of them even think it's a temple."

There was an excited prickling at the back of my neck, a dull but hopeful flutter deep in my chest and stomach, but I did my best not to give anything away. The journalist knew too much already. She certainly didn't need me giving her anything more. "That's interesting" I said. "But the Council has a complete catalog of possible temple locations, as does the MCDC, and there's nothing in either of them about Lowell."

"Which means what, Councilor? That the Council's omniscient now? That it's infallible? That the MCDC never fucks shit up? I think we both know that none of those things are true."

As she talked, I tried to recall what little I knew about Lowell Crater. It was an old settlement, one of the first, but a couple of fusion warheads dropped from orbit just after the start of the war had all but destroyed it. When the dust settled, after treaties had been signed and the plagues had finally burned themselves out, the Transit Authority had decided what was left at Lowell would make a good last stop before the South Pole. And that's about all that I could recall, and none of it suggested that the Fenrir would choose Lowell as a temple site.

"Assuming you're not just yanking this out of your ass, Ms. Vaughn, why hasn't MBS released this information? Why hasn't the TA already filed disclosure reports with the MCDC and Offworld Control?"

"Ask them," she said, staring up at the ceiling of the cabin now. *Maybe that's where they hid the other cameras,* I thought, not caring how paranoid I'd become. "My guess," she continued, "they're afraid the military's gonna come sweeping in to clear the place out, and they'll lose a base they can't afford to lose, the economy being what it is. It'd cost them a fortune to relocate—"

"And what about the network?"

"The network?" she asked, looking at me again. "Well, we just want to be sure of our sources. No sense broadcasting stories that might cause a panic and have severe pecuniary consequences, if there's a chance it's all just something dreamed up by a few bored mechs stuck in some shithole at the bottom of the world. MBS will release the story, when we're ready. Maybe you'll be a part of it, Councilor, before this thing is done."

And then she stood up, thanked me for my time, and walked back to her assigned seat nearer the front of the passenger cabin. I sat alone, silently repeating all the things she'd said, hearing her voice in my head—*But they've seen some things. Some of them even think it's a temple.* Outside the airship's protective womb, night was quickly claiming the high plains of the Sun, and I could just make out the irregular red-orange silhouette of Phobos rising—or so it seemed—above the western horizon.

It took me another two weeks to reach Lowell. The commercial airships don't run that far south, and I deplaned at Holden (noting that Ariadne Vaughn did not) and then spent four days trying to find someone willing to transport me the two thousand-plus kilometers south and west to Bosporos City. From there, I hoped to buy a nook on the TA line the rest of the way down to Lowell.

Finally, I paid a platinum prospector half of what was left in my accounts to make the trip. She grumbled endlessly about pirates and dust sinks, about the wear and mileage the trip would put on her rusted-out crawler. But it was likely more money than she'd see in the next three or four years cracking rocks and tagging cores, and we only broke down once, when the aft sediment filter clogged and the engine overheated. I had a narrow, filthy bunk behind the Laskar coils, and spent much of the trip asleep or watching the monotonous terrain roll by outside the windows. To the east, there were occasional, brief glimpses of shadowed canyonlands which I knew lead down to the wide, empty expanse of the Argyre Planitia laid out almost six klicks below the surrounding plains. I considered the possibility that *it* might be the corpse-strewn crater from my dreams, this monstrous wound carved deep into the face of Mars almost four thousand million years ago during the incessant bombardments of the Noachian Age, when the solar system was still young and hot and violent.

That thought only made the nightmares worse, of course. I considered asking the prospector to find another route, one that would not have taken us so close to the canyons, but I knew she'd only laugh her bitter laugh, start in on dust sinks again, and tell me to go to hell. So I didn't say anything.

Instead, I lay listening to the stones being ground to powder beneath the crawler's treads, to the wind battering itself against the hull, to the old-womanish wheeze of the failing Laskar coils, trying not to remember the thing Mikaela had shown me beneath Hope VII or what I might yet find in the ruins of Lowell. I slept, and I dreamed.

And on the final afternoon before we reached Bosporos City, dreaming, I made my way at last to the center of the crater. There was a desperate, lightless crawl through the mummified

intestines of some leviathan while the Fenrir's pipes and strings
and drums pounded at my senses. My ears and nose were bleeding when I emerged through a gaping tear in the creature's gut
and stood, half-blind, blinking up at towering ebony spires and
soaring arches and stairways that seemed to reach almost all the
way to the stars. The music poured from this black city, gushed
from every window and open doorway, and I sank to my knees
and cried.

"You weren't ever meant to come here," Sailor said, and I
realized she was standing over me. "You weren't invited."

"I can't *do* this shit anymore," I sobbed, for once not caring if
she saw my weakness. "I can't."

"You never should have started."

My tears turned to crystal and fell with a sound like wind
chimes. My heart turned to cut glass in my chest.

"Is this what you were looking for?" I asked her, gazing up at
the spires and arches, hating that cruel, singing architecture, even
as my soul begged it to open up and swallow me alive.

"No. This is only a dream, Dorry," she said, speaking to me
as she might a child. "*You* made this place. You've been building
it all your life."

"No. That's not true," I replied, though I understood perfectly
well that it was, that it *must* be. The distance across the corpse-
littered crater was only half the diameter of my own damnation,
nothing more.

"If I let you see, will go back?" she asked. "Will you go back
and forget me?" She was speaking very softly, but I had no trouble
hearing her over the wind and the music and the wheezing Laskar
coils. I must have answered, must have said yes, because she took my
hand in hers, and the black city before us collapsed and dissolved,
taking the music with it, and I stood, instead, on a low platform
in what I at first mistook for a room. But then I saw the fleshy,
pulsing walls, the purple-green interlace of veins and capillaries,
the massive supporting ribs or ridges, blacker than the vanished
city, dividing that place into seven unequal crescent chambers.

I stood somewhere within a living thing, within something that dwarfed even the fallen giants from the crater.

And each of the crescent chambers contained the remains of a single gray pilgrim, their bodies metamorphosed over months or years or decades to serve the needs of this incomplete, demonic biology. They were each no more than appendages now, human beings become coalesced obligate parasites or symbiotes, their glinting, chitinous bodies all but lost in a labyrinth of mucosal membranes, buried by the array of connective tissues and tubes that sprouted from them like cancerous umbilical cords.

Anglerfish. Is it one word or two?

And there, half buried in the chamber walls, was what remained of Sailor, just enough left of her face that I could be sure it was her. Something oily and red and viscous that wasn't blood leaked from the hole that had been her mouth, from the wreck of her lips and teeth, her mouth become only one more point of exit or entry for the restless, palpitating cords connecting her with this enormous organism. Her eyes opened partway, those atrophied slits opening to reveal bright, wet orbs like pools of night, and the fat, segmented tube emerging from the gap of her thighs began to quiver violently.

Can you see me now, Dorry? she whispered, her voice burrowing in behind my eyes, filled with pain and joy and regret beyond all comprehension. *Have you seen enough? Or do you need to see more?*

"No," I told her, waking up, opening my eyes wide and vomiting onto the floor beneath my bunk. The Laskar coils had stopped wheezing, and the crawler was no longer moving. I rolled over and lay very still, cold and sick and sweating, staring up at the dingy, low ceiling until the prospector finally came looking for me.

When I left home back in Aries, I brought the monk's book with me, the book from Sailor's crate of discards. I sit here on my bedroll in one corner of one room inside the concrete and steel husk of a bombed-out Federal compound in Lowell. I have come this far, and I am comforted by the knowledge that there's only a little ways left to go. I open the book and read the words aloud again, the words underlined in red ink, that I might understand how not to lose my way in this tale which is almost all that remains of me: "No story has a beginning, and no story has an end. Beginnings and endings may be conceived to serve a purpose, to serve a momentary and transient intent, but they are, in their truer nature, arbitrary and exist solely as a construct of the mind of man."

I think this means I can stop when I'm ready.

I've been in Lowell for almost a full week now, writing all this shit down. Today is Monday, Libra 17th. We are so deep in winter, and I have never been this far south.

There is a silence here, in this dead city, that seems almost as solid as the bare concrete around me. I'm camped far enough in from the transfer station that the hanger noise, the comings and goings of the zeps and spinners, the clockwork opening and closing of the dome, seem little more than a distant, occasional thunder. I'm not sure I've ever known such a profound silence as this. Were I sane, it might drive me mad. There *are* sounds, sounds other than the far-off noise of the station, but they are petty things that only seem to underscore the silence. They're more like the too-often recollected *memory* of sound, an ancient woman deaf since childhood remembering what sound was like before she lost it forever.

Last night, I lay awake, fighting sleep, listening to my heart and all those other petty sounds. I dozed towards dawn, and when I woke there was a woman crouched a few feet from my bedroll. She was reading the monk's book, flipping the pages in the dark, and, at first, I thought I was dreaming again, that this was another dream of Sailor. But then she closed the book and looked at me. Even in the dark, I could tell she wasn't as young as Sailor, and I saw that her head was shaved down to the skin. Her eyes were iridescent and flashed blue-green in the gloom.

"May I switch on the light?" I asked, pointing towards the travel lamp near my pillow.

"If you wish," she replied and set the book back down among my things. "If you need it."

I touched the lamp, and it blinked obediently on, throwing long shadows against the walls and floor and ceiling of the room where I was sleeping. The woman squinted, cursed, and turned her face away. I rubbed at my own eyes and sat up.

"What do you want?" I asked her.

"We saw you, yesterday. You were watching."

The woman was a Fenrir priest. She wore the signs on her skin and ragged clothing. Her feet were bare, and there was a simple onyx ring on each of her toes. I could tell that she'd been very beautiful once.

"Yes," I told her. "I was watching."

"But you didn't come for the mark," she said, not asking because she already knew the answer. "You came to find someone."

"Does that happen very often?"

She turned her face towards me again, shading her eyes with her left hand. "Do you think you will find her, Dorry? Do you think you'll take her back?"

It hadn't been hard to locate the temple. The old Federal complex lies near the center of the dome, what the bombs left of it, anyway, and finding it was really no more than a matter of walking. The day that I arrived in Lowell City, one of the Transfer Authority's security agents had detained and questioned me for an hour or so, and I'd assured her that I was there as a scholar, looking for records that might have survived the war. I'd shown her the paper map that I'd purchased at a bookshop in Bosporos and pointed out the black X I'd made about half a mile north of the feddy, near one of the old canals. She'd looked at the map two or three times, asked me a few questions about the journey down from Holden, and then made a call to her senior officer before releasing me.

"You don't want to go down that way," she'd told me, tapping the map with an index finger. "I can't hold you here or deport you,

Councilor. But you better trust me on this, you don't want to go down there."

"You've been chasing her such a long time," the woman crouched on the floor before me said, speaking more quietly now and smiling. Her teeth were filed to sharp points, and she licked at them with the tip of her violet tongue. "You must have had a lot of chances to give up. There must have been so much despair."

"Is she dead?" I asked, the words slipping almost nonsensically from my lips.

"No one *dies*. You know that. You've known that since the camp. No one ever dies."

"You know where she is?"

"She's with the wolf," the woman whispered. "Three weeks now, she's with the wolf. You came too late, Dorry. You came to her too late," and she drew a knife from her belt, something crude and heavy fashioned from scrap metal. "She isn't waiting anymore."

I kicked her hard, the toe of my right boot catching her in the chest just below her collar bone, and the priest cried out and fell over backwards. The knife slipped from her fingers and skittered away across the concrete.

"Did the wolf tell *you* that you'd never die?" I demanded, getting to my feet and aiming the pistol at her head. I'd bought that in Bosporos, as well, the same day I'd bought the map, black-market military picked up cheap in the backroom of a britch bar. The blinking green ready light behind the sight assured me that the safety was off, that the trip cells were hot, and there was a live charge in the chamber. The woman coughed and clutched at her chest, then spat something dark onto the floor.

"That's what I want to know, bitch," I said, "what I want you to *tell* me," and I kicked her in the ribs. She grunted and tried to crawl away, so I kicked her again, harder than before, and she stopped moving. "I want you to tell me if that's what it *promised* you, that you'd fucking get to live forever if you brought it whatever it needed. Because I want *you* to know that it fucking lied."

And she opened her mouth wide, then, and I caught a glimpse of the barbed thing uncoiling from the hollow beneath her tongue and pulled the trigger.

I suspect that one gunshot was the loudest noise anyone's heard here since the day bombs fell on Lowell. It echoed off the thick walls, all that noise trapped in such a little room, and left my ears ringing painfully. The priest was dead, and I sat down on my bedroll again. I'd never imagined that there would be so much blood or that killing someone could be so very simple. No, that's not true. I've imagined it all along.

I've been sitting here on the roof for the last hour, watching as the domeworks begin to mimic the morning light, shivering while the frost clinging to the old masonry melts away as the solar panels warm the air of Lowell. I brought the monk's book with me and half a bottle of whiskey and the gun. And my notebook, to write the last of it down.

When the bottle is empty, maybe then I'll make a decision. Maybe then I'll know what comes next.

I'd show them the stars
And the meaning of life
They'd shut me away
But I'd be all right
All right...
                    —Radiohead

Afterword

By Elizabeth Bear

I think part of the power of literature is that almost everyone, somewhere in their secret heart, has wondered about two things. First, what would it be like to be someone—or *something*—else, to experience the world with different senses and preconceptions? And second, *how do we look from the outside?*

For reader or writer, engaging with a book or story can serve as a means of imagining how someone else might intersect with the world. And—more rare and precious (and occasionally appalling)— sometimes it can give the reader a sense of standing beside herself and looking in, as if through glass. The observation window of a dissectionist's theater. The cover slip of a microscopic slide.

Addressing that second and challenging question has been a preoccupation of genre horror and science fiction, all the way back to their roots in Mary Shelley's *Frankenstein: or, The Modern Prometheus.* In that most famous of Gothic novels, Shelley confronts themes of alienation and the alien monstrousness of human nature that have become an essential part of the speculative fiction discourse, and the spring from which some of our despised genre's most powerful work is sourced.

In such works, bleakness and inexorability, the grinding glacial logic of a measureless and unresonant universe, pale in their horror beside merely human failings. Nature and space may be cold, vast, and awesome…but even beside their terrors, it is in the pettiness, the *mereness*, of human nature that true horror lies.

What I mean is that *Frankenstein* as a Gothic is a transitional form, because in *Frankenstein*, the traditional Gothic trope of the innocent overtaken by corruption is subverted. Because the innocent in *Frankenstein* is the monster, and the title character—Victor Frankenstein—carries within him the spot from which corruption grows.

And speculative fiction, a blossom sprung from the seed that Mary Shelley planted, accepts as a genre that what we mean when we say *human* is a romanticization, and that the monsters—the true monsters—are not the horrors of deep space or the wolf at the door, but us.

Just us.

That realization—of human monstrosity—informs the work of H. P. Lovecraft. As he wrote, "If we knew what we are, we should do as Sir Arthur Jermyn did; and Arthur Jermyn soaked himself in oil and set fire to his clothing one night."

The idea that the romantic ideations in which we cloak ourselves are only comforting lies is a strong pulse in speculative fiction's disquieting heart. Among others, you can find it (historically) in the work of Arthur C. Clarke, of Theodore Sturgeon, of John Brunner, of Andre Norton, of James Tiptree, Jr; and more recently in the work of Robert Charles Wilson, Peter Watts…and Caitlín R. Kiernan.

I once had a series of conversations with Peter Watts and Chelsea Polk (another Canadian SF writer), and in which we coined the term "eco-Gothic" to describe that particular sensibility, the one that informs the work of writers who grew up on Lovecraft and Brunner. These writers understand that humanity's purported importance to the universe is but solipsism, and that the human species, rather than following any manifest destiny, is merely a struggling spark in a vast Darwinian sea of night.

I know that Caitlín herself has adopted the term, so I have no hesitation at all in applying it to her work, in all its bleak gorgeousness. This is eco-Gothic, a sensibility in modern science fiction that has grown from the (Gothic-informed but forward-looking) work of Mary Shelley, spread tendrils through Lovecraft and Brunner, and found fruit and dark flower here, in these stories collected in the book you hold in your hand.

But Caitlín in not simply a purveyor of fashionable bleakness. What Caitlín has created in *A is for Alien* is a sort of fugue composed of related stories that confront this trope quite squarely, and the effect is a disquieting, alienating beauty that provides a suite of answers to that second question—what do we look like from outside?

The bleakness of Caitlín's world is not merely the bleakness of an uncaring universe. It's the bleakness of human futility. Caitlín's world is God-forsaken, in every sense of the term. But as the poet Richard Brautigan once wrote, "God-forsaken is beautiful, too."

Her nihilism is surreal, dreamlike, and the surrealness—the dreamscape difficulty—of her work provides a great deal of the alienation that is such an effective part of her technique.

In Lovecraft, as in the Gothic novel (setting apart, for the moment, *Frankenstein*, because this is one of the ways in which it does not conform to the Gothic model), the past wells up to consume and drown the present, crashing it under and drowning it like the deep implacable sea which he fills with such terrors. But in Caitlín's work, it is not the past from which we struggle to escape. Not the monsters out of the id or out of time, the ancient unevolved horrors that still dwell within us. It is ourselves, our social personas, our constructed realities. The despair in these stories of Caitlín's is both a Lovecraftian despair—the monster we struggle to escape from is within us, is part and parcel of our genes, is inextricable by any surgeon's knife from our DNA—and an evolution of Lovecraft. Because in these stories, a transformation into other—what Caitlín terms a "species of one"—is the path out of that horror.

Even if that path leads through mutilation and death.

There is nothing more alien in the world inside this collection than the narrators themselves.

In these pages, Caitlín quotes Sidonie-Gabrielle Colette, who wrote, "Look for a long time at what pleases you, and for a longer time at what pains you." It reminds me of one of my favorite quotations, from Akira Kurosawa, who is reported to have said, "To be an artist means to never avert your eyes."

Art is about honesty. As artists, we choose what we show; we are deceivers at the heart. But we must lie with intent to reveal, not to mislead, or our art is a travesty. And so when Caitlín introduces you to these encounters with the alien, bear this in mind. No matter what she shows you, the fabulous horrors of possession, gestation, conversion, contagion, infection, adulteration of the self in all its forms—the men and women who willingly open themselves to transformation by (into?) machine, virus, alien, beast, piece of art—she's holding up a mirror. She suggests that transformation—that evolution—is perhaps, no matter how terrifying and horrific it may seem—the only path to survival in (or escape from) a world that has become too terrible to endure.

She presents a world in which we may have to become grotesque in order to survive...but then, were we not grotesque already, under the makeup and the denial?

Caitlín is not insensible to the impact of that transformation on those left behind, however, or on those who try and fail. She looks hard at these displeasing things, and she chooses not to avert her eyes. In the process, she brings her readers on a journey through dreamlike and terrible lands, through misery and wonder, to the ends of human endurance. She invites us to inspect what lies under our despised human shells, and understand that the failed transformations are the most terrible—as if through glass. The observation window of a dissectionist's theater. The cover slip of a microscopic slide.

She shows us that we are the monsters. Far more monstrous than our creations. Frankenstein and his creature, the corruptor and the innocent.

You are the alien. And from the outside, how strange you seem to me.

About the Author

Trained as a vertebrate paleontologist, Caitlín R. Kiernan did not turn to fiction writing until 1992. Since then, she has published six novels—*The Five of Cups, Silk, Threshold, Low Red Moon, Murder of Angels,* and, most recently, *Daughter of Hounds.* Her short fiction has been collected in *Tales of Pain and Wonder; Wrong Things* (with Poppy Z. Brite); *From Weird and Distant Shores;* the World Fantasy award-nominated *To Charles Fort, With Love;* and *Alabaster.* She has also published a short sf novel, *The Dry Salvages,* and two volumes of erotica, *Frog Toes and Tentacles* and *Tales from the Woeful Platypus.* She has scripted graphic novels for DC Vertigo, including thirty-eight issues of *The Dreaming* and the mini-series *The Girl Who Would Be Death* and *Bast: Eternity Game.* Her many chapbooks have included *Trilobite: The Writing of Threshold, The Merewife,* and *The Black Alphabet.* She is currently working on her next novel, *The Red Tree.* Her first sf story, "Between the Flatirons and the Deep Green Sea," was published in 1995.

About the Artist

Vince Locke grew up in Michigan. He studied commercial art at Eastern Michigan University, but left after two years to work on *Deadworld*. He has been lucky enough to work on such graphic novels as *The Sandman* and *A History of Violence* (later filmed by director David Cronenberg). He has been warping kids' minds for over twenty-five years as the cover artist for the death-metal band Cannibal Corpse. He has also provided the illustrations for Caitlín R. Kiernan's *Frog Toes and Tentacles* and *Tales from the Woeful Platypus*, and, since 2005, has been the regular illustrator for her monthly *Sirenia Digest*. Most of his subject matter is on the dark side, but also veers towards the strange and beautiful. He still lives in Michigan with his wife and two sons.